AND BABY MAKES FOUR

MARY J. FORBES

Silhouette®

SPECIAL EDITION®

Published by Silhouette Books

America's Publisher of Contemporary Romance

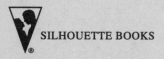

SILHOUETTE BOOKS

ISBN-13: 978-0-373-24938-1
ISBN-10:   0-373-24938-1

AND BABY MAKES FOUR

Books by Mary J. Forbes

Silhouette Special Edition

A Forever Family #1625
A Father, Again #1661
Everything She's Ever Wanted #1702
Twice Her Husband #1755
The Man from Montana #1800
His Brother's Gift #1840
Red Wolf's Return #1858
First-Time Valentine #1881
†*Their Secret Child* #1902
†*And Baby Makes Four* #1938

*The Wilder Family
†Home to Firewood Island

MARY J. FORBES

Her rural prairie roots granted Mary J. Forbes a deep love of nature and small towns, a love that's often reflected in the settings of her books. Today, she lives with her family in the Pacific Northwest where she also teaches school, nurtures her garden and walks or jogs in any weather. Readers can contact Mary at www.maryjforbes.com.

With many thanks to my editor, Susan Litman

Chapter One

The man stood watching her in the early-April twilight.

Had he been alone, Lee Tait might have worried. This was, after all, the third time in as many days he stopped to observe her tinker on the Cessna 206 seaplane docked at the end of the boardwalk that curved within Burnt Bend's tiny cove. As before, the child accompanied him, a boy of perhaps six or seven whose dusty blond hair caught the sun's setting rays. His eyes, Lee noted, were plate-round with curiosity.

Still, the guy's presence—yet again—couldn't stop the cold sluice of adrenaline down her torso. What did he want? Why didn't he continue along the shoreline path, which extended from the marina and wended past a smattering of cottages before looping back into the village, a distance of a quarter mile?

Why stop each time to stare at her for five minutes, and then turn around?

He stood in the fading light, rangy as a mountain climber, attired in gray cords, brown boat shoes and a black pullover. Except for a pair of gym shoes, the child emulated the dress code.

Obviously, father and son.

Two peas in a pod, her mother would say—if Lee explained the strange visitations to Charmaine. Which she would not.

The boy murmured something and, while low and indistinct, she heard the man's quiet response drift down the wooden dock.

Trying to avoid the duo, she opened the seaplane's door, stepped on the pontoon and hopped inside for a final check before tomorrow's flight across the Puget Sound.

Last fall, she had signed a year's contract with the Burnt Bend post office to courier expedited mail and parcels to the mainland. The daily service ensured a steady paycheck, while weekend visitors and tourists to the region kept her fledgling charter company viable. One day soon—when she could afford rising fuel costs—she hoped to include a scheduled weekday passenger service.

Lee winced at the thought. Cutting into Lucien Duvall's passengers-only ferry service would not make the old guy happy.

Hopefully, when the time came, they'd be able to work something out.

Scanning for forgotten items left by passengers, she thought how the Cessna was the only good thing to come from her ex-husband. She hadn't selected the best of his Abner Air fleet out of spite, or because he'd impregnated that cocktail waitress three years ago.

Then again, maybe she had....

Truth was, she'd picked the six-seater seaplane as the cornerstone of Sky Dash, a company she'd dreamed of founding since her twentieth birthday.

Spotting a crumpled island brochure under the farthest passenger seat, Lee recalled her last customer clutching the pamphlet in a death grip. *Ah, well.* Edgy fliers came with the territory.

Reaching down, she snagged the leaflet.

"Hello, there," a deep voice said from behind.

Snapping around, she bumped her head on the cockpit's ceiling.

She hadn't heard him approach, but there he and the boy stood on the weathered pier, gazing at her rump in army-green coveralls, no less, as she leaned over the seat.

Swell. The guy wanted a tête-à-tête now? While her backside hung in his face?

Ignoring the warmth climbing her neck, she scrambled into the pilot's seat.

"Hey," she said, as if they hadn't seen each other three times at precisely 6:30 p.m. in the past seventy-two hours. *Be friendly, Lee. He could be a future weekend fare.*

His eyes held humor. "Are you Amelia Earhart the Second?"

"I'm Lee Tait," she stated, a little irked the guy would zero in on a nickname the townsfolk had given her when she received her wings fifteen years ago. "Owner and pilot of Sky Dash."

"Sorry, ma'am." He looked askance as if another thought chased through his mind. Then, with the boy close to his side, he offered a handshake. "Nice to meet you, Captain Tait."

She leaned out the door. His grip was firm, large. A frisson of electricity shot up her arm. "No apology needed." *I'm used to the nickname.* "And you are…?"

Shaking his head, he issued a short laugh. "I'm losing it. Rogan Matteo."

"Rogan." She tested the name, found it oddly pleasing. But…something niggled. Where had she heard his last name…?

He had quiet, gray eyes and soot-black hair. Although his voice suggested the South, his face revealed a none-too-genteel life. A nose too brash to be handsome, a square, tough jaw and cheekbones embracing the genes of a Spanish ancestor. Not handsome, yet appealing in a rudimentary sense.

Disregarding a scurry of nerves at how his eyes imprisoned hers, Lee jumped out of the plane. On the dock, she saw he was taller than she assumed; she could lay her head on his chest, if she chose.

Shaking off the image, she closed the seaplane's door and picked up her metal toolbox. "What can I do for you, Mr. Matteo?" she asked, starting down the floating dock toward the boardwalk and its array of quaint stores and food outlets.

"I understand you make daily flights to the mainland."

"I courier the island's critical mail Monday through Friday."

"Do you take passengers on those runs?"

"Sometimes. However, it depends on their destination and schedule. If I'm flying mail and we're going in the same direction and at the same time, passengers are welcome."

"Are they welcome at other times during the day?"

She stopped. They were at the junction of her dock and the boardwalk, and the boy held his dad's hand.

"Of course," she said. "As long as I'm back on time if there's a mail run."

"Ah." Matteo gazed momentarily across the water where the sun sank below the horizon, leaving a blood-stain on the ocean. Glancing down at the boy, his eyes softened; on her they were all business. "In a week or so, I'll need temporary shuttling to Renton, Captain Tait. Three, four days at most. My son's attending the elementary school here, so I need to be back in time to pick him up."

"What's wrong with Lu's foot ferry?" she asked. Let Lucien Duvall take the man on his sixty-passenger water taxi. It made three daily trips.

"Nothing's wrong with his ferry, but you stop at Renton, which means I can walk to work. Lu docks at Seattle, and he leaves at 7:30 a.m. with a five-thirty return. Your eight and three o'clock schedules fit my son—" another glance at the boy "—and me better."

My son and me. Did that mean the child's mother lived elsewhere? Oddly, the notion of a wife waiting in the wings sent a shaft of disappointment through Lee.

"I'm willing to pay the going rate," Matteo went on.

Unable to withhold her amazement, Lee blinked. Temporary or not, a week of daily return flights would cost him. Either he or his company had money. Since he was a stranger to the island—she knew practically every one of its two thousand souls—she'd bet he was the one with money. Probably another of the rich who came to Firewood Island looking for a chunk of so-called "nature," while building a mansion with an ocean view.

Although the idea bothered her, where he built his home had nothing to do with her hesitancy. She did not wish to be near him. He was a man with a child. A man who could make her heart skip with a simple *hello, there*.

Her no-nonsense black shoes clicking against the wood, she started for the apartment she rented above Art Smarts, a whimsical shop catering to the island's artsy community.

Matteo took the heavy toolbox from her grip. "Do you always maintain your own plane?"

"Every day." She noticed he carried the toolbox easily, and wondered if he was always a gentleman. Her heart beat a little harder.

"So, you're a mechanic, too?" he asked with that Southern inflection.

"Not officially, but over the years I've learned a few things about plane engines." *Most of it from my ex who owns a charter airline.* "Don't worry, Mr. Matteo," she said, mentally batting Stuart Hershel out of her mind. "I hire a professional to overhaul my plane twice a year."

Halting again, she retrieved the toolkit from his grip. Suddenly, she didn't like his questions. And she certainly didn't like that she noticed too much about him, which vexed her even more, especially after his scrutiny of the last three days.

"I could probably help with your situation," she went on. "However, I won't be responsible for getting you to work on time. If something goes wrong and I'm late, you'll be late. And vice versa. If something holds you up here or on the mainland, I can't wait for you."

He held up a hand. "I understand. However, I've checked your flight history. Since you were hired by the post office seven months ago, you haven't missed a day or a time. Nor have you missed your other fares." His smile canted left. "I'm a lawyer, Miss Lee. Comprehensive research comes with the job."

A lawyer. Who'd had her investigated. What else had he discovered? A chill spilled through her bones. Three years ago, she had returned to her hometown to escape a past that haunted her nights.

He dug a card from a hip pocket. "Call anytime and we'll set up a schedule. I don't go to bed until eleven."

She studied the print. *Rogan B. Matteo, Law Offices of Matteo and Matteo.* Address: Renton, where she often docked. Was he part of a husband-and-wife team?

He said, "I'm having a new one printed up this week, but the cell phone number will stay the same."

"Sure," she said. Intent on reaching her apartment, and trying to shake off his magnetism, she hurried down the boardwalk. All right, she would admit the man seemed like a nice guy. But then lawyers were always nice guys—when they were on your side.

"Thank you," he called. "By the way, in case you want to reach me, I'm renting a cabin at The Country Cabin B and B until our new house is ready."

Her sister's place. "Why am I not surprised?" Lee muttered. Kat operated the prettiest, best-priced B and B on the island.

So. Not only had Rogan Matteo spent the better part

of the weekend tailing Lee, he had installed himself in Kat's life, too. Two sisters with one stone, so to speak.

Fine. Two could play that game. In a couple hours, while she shared Sunday dinner with her sister, Lee would dig out some information about Lawyer Matteo and those dollars he was willing to dole out like Halloween candy. Dollars Lee could use to safeguard Sky Dash and ensure her plane stayed in the air.

She would not, absolutely would not, reflect on how or why he made her fingers tingle and her breath quicken.

Rogan tucked the blankets around his son's shoulders. "Catch you in the morning, Dan-the-Man." Leaning in, he kissed the boy's forehead. After coming home from the dock and the bath/cookie/milk/bedtime story ritual completed, it was time for lights out.

"'Night, Daddy." Yawning, Danny turned to the wall.

Clicking off the bedside lamp, Rogan started for the door.

The sheets swished. "Dad? Are you really gonna fly in that lady's plane?"

Rogan returned to the bed to sit at his son's hip. "Yeah, buddy, I am. I don't like you being with a sitter so long after school."

What he couldn't say was he didn't like the idea of a stranger watching over his child, even though the sitter was a respected woman in the community whose livelihood had been caring for kids after school for almost thirty years. Hell, she came with an arm's length of glowing reports and references—all of which he'd checked thoroughly.

But Daniel was his remaining child. Rogan had given too many extra hours to his career when Darby and little Sophie still lived. That mistake had been more costly than he could fathom, and one he would never repeat.

"But," Danny whispered, "aren't you scared?"

Of flying. Rogan gently squeezed his child's hand. "Truth?"

A quick nod.

"Sort of," he admitted. "However, I can't let it stop me from going to work, son. Or from getting into a plane. Yes, sometimes things are scary, but we can't let them control what we need to do. Ms. Tait will save me a lot of time with her plane." *And I need to show you that fears can be overcome, that you don't need to be afraid for the rest of your life.*

"Is her plane safe?"

"Yes. It is. She gets it checked regularly."

Still, Rogan's stomach clenched. Every day he thanked all the deities for the earache that had kept Danny from boarding that fated flight. But, oh God, why had he not listened to Darby's intuition? Why had he pushed his wife to make that journey back to the City of Forks for her mother's sixtieth birthday?

The morning of the flight had been foggy. *I don't feel good about this, Rogan,* she'd said, and he'd replied, *It'll be fine. You'll be there before you know it. I'll call you at lunch, okay?*

But she and Sophie, their eight-year-old daughter, had never made it to Forks. And now he was putting a case together against the airline company.

He stroked his son's hair. "We've talked about this, remember? Dad's opening his own office here on the island. Then I'll never have to leave home again, and when I am at the office I'll be practically around the corner from your school. Flying with Captain Tait is not forever. Just a few days this week, and maybe next. Just until Uncle Johnny and I get things settled at the old office."

"Why can't Uncle Johnny move here, too?"

Rogan sighed. "Because he likes the big city." Although Johnny would never admit it, Rogan believed the fast life was his younger brother's validation as the family rebel, a label their parents had hung on him at fifteen.

On the pillow, the boy curled a hand under his cheek. "Promise you'll come back?"

"I promise."

Silence. Then, "Maybe that's why Mommy never came back. She didn't promise."

"Oh, Danny. No one expects bad things to happen." *It's always the other guy who's unlucky.*

"You mean if she'd promised she'd be alive now?"

"No, buddy. Promises don't mean bad things won't happen."

"But you just promised."

"Shove over, okay?" Rogan lay down beside his child and pulled him into a hug. "Promises are sort of like agreements. They mean you'll do your best to fulfill them. But once in a while things get in the way…and the agreement is broken."

"Like the mountain got in the way of Mom and Sophie's plane?"

"Yeah." Rogan closed his eyes on a flash of pain. "Sort of."

"Are there mountains between here and Renton?"

Mount Rainier. "Not one we'll be flying over."

A quiet fell. "Okay," came the soft reply.

"You about ready to sleep now, pal?"

"Hmm. 'Night, Dad."

"'Night, tiger."

Rogan eased from the mattress. He pulled the door to a five-inch gap and headed for the cabin's living room. Shrugging into a wool-lined vest, he stepped quietly out the door and onto the tiny front porch. Beyond the trees, the ocean swooshed against the shore with the rhythm of a metronome.

He liked the cabin, liked the secluded woods, away from the old Victorian that was the main house. Here he could think without the interruption of other guests or the owner/hostess, Kat O'Brien, and her son. Not that he didn't like the single mother. He did; she had given him a respectable two-week deal while he waited for his recently purchased farmhouse to undergo repairs and reconstruction.

Thinking of the ninety-year-old structure a mile from town, Rogan smiled. Farmhouse, indeed. Once, long ago, it had overlooked a sixty-acre sheep farm. Today, the acres totaled fifteen and contained a house and barn in dire need of paint and repairs and a mare with a three-week-old foal.

Taking Danny to see the horses had cinched the deal. One look at that fuzzy-chinned baby gamboling beside its great-bellied mother, and the boy had been a goner.

I wanna live here, Daddy, and pet the baby horse every day.

After a thousand tears and months of heartbreak following the deaths of his wife and daughter, Rogan hadn't been able to refuse the boy anything. Not even a farm. So he'd bought the place, hired the island handyman Zeb Jantz to do enough repairs to make it livable, and moved from Renton to this B and B cabin in order to settle Dan into the elementary school as well as oversee the renovation.

But on nights like this…nights when his little guy questioned Darby's crash, Rogan wanted nothing more than to turn back the clock three years to the exact moment he had booked that charter flight to Forks. And the moment he heard Darby's premonition. He'd cancel the flight and tell her to stay home.

He'd say he loved her *one more time.*

Scratching his stubbled cheeks, he sat on one of the porch's two wicker chairs. The spice of sea clung to the night's breeze and stars glittered like crushed glass in the sky.

He wasn't sure how long he sat there, listening and waiting for what he didn't know, before the *ping-ping* of the cell phone on his belt shot through his musings. Caller ID indicated a text message from his younger brother in Renton, where Rogan had once lived with Darby and set up a law office with Johnny.

Hey guy, the message began. *Hope ur not in the sack.* Rogan's mouth lifted into a smile as he checked the watch at his wrist and realized that already an hour had passed. "Time flies when you're having fun," he muttered. He continued to read: *Got some news re case. Need 2 discuss. Tomoro at 9 work 4 u? jkm*

Tomorrow? That meant contacting Lee Tait tonight and flying in her floatplane well before he'd planned. Before he had a week to psych himself up for the ordeal.

Because as much as he pretended otherwise, for him flying *would* be an ordeal.

Cant u call now? he wrote. Within sixty seconds he had an answer: *In L8 meet. See u tomoro.* Rogan grunted. He could imagine Johnny's late meeting. No doubt it involved a long-legged blonde.

Contemplating, he replied, *Ill call u at 9.* He did not want to get on that plane this soon.

No, came the return. *B HERE at 9!*

Rogan stared at the message. What the hell could be so important that they had to meet in person?

With a sigh he shut the phone. One way or another, he'd find out tomorrow. He only hoped it was something positive in the suit he was building against the charter airline company that killed his family.

Don't think of that now, he thought, staring at the night sky with its canopy of stars. *Or you won't get to sleep tonight.*

He forced himself to relax. Three hundred yards away, the ocean lapped against the shore and he turned his memories to his encounters with Lee Tait a few hours before.

Her womanly charms surprised him. All that red hair in a thick wavy tail trailing down her back, and those eyes, green as the budding leaves on the farm....

The freckles across her skin had surprised him further. At a distance she appeared pale and thin, but within arm's length her complexion glowed like the setting sun, and her shape had the litheness of a willow.

But what caught him most was the heat in his groin when his name tumbled from her lips in a voice made for the night.

Shame slashed through him. How could he think of another woman? Darby had been the love of his life for seventeen years. No one could replace her.

Shoulders lifting on an extensive breath, he returned to the wicker chair. Slouching forward, he shoved his hands into his hair.

He was so goddamned tired. Tired of the loneliness, of hurting and grieving, and wishing time was reversible. He needed to move on, really move on. For Danny and for himself. Living like a monk wasn't the answer.

And Johnny was right. Hiding on an island wasn't the answer, either. Because no matter how hard Rogan tried, the memories dragged along like tattered old blankets. Well, right or wrong he'd made the choice, and next week he'd hang out his shingle. But first, he needed to cajole the lovely Lee into taking him tomorrow in that confined little seaplane.

He looked toward the bed-and-breakfast. He had her business number from her Sky Dash Web site. He could call her, except two hours ago he'd seen her drive up in a red Jeep and go into the Victorian. Another surprise. Did she live here, rent a room?

He could call the main desk and ask for her extension.

Or he could wait until morning, talk to her face-to-face on the wharf, hand her a wad of bills she couldn't refuse.

For the first time in years, his heart pounded with anticipation.

Chapter Two

Lee's sister, Kat, cut a wedge of dessert and lifted it onto her plate.

"I can't believe you're refusing my apple crumble," she groused. Dinner done, the dishes washed, they sat in the living room of Kat's B and B, while her son finished a school assignment in his bedroom. "Are you sick or something?"

Lee shrugged. "Lately I haven't been very hungry." In reality, she'd been a tad woozy now and again during the past month, which could be a symptom for a dozen ailments. A stomach bug, eating the wrong food….

Except, she couldn't remember the last time she had the flu. But she knew exactly when she'd last had a bout of *evening* wooziness.

Five years ago, when she'd been pregnant with Stuart's baby.

Damn it, she was *not* pregnant. This was a bug she'd caught from one of her weekend passengers or Kat's son, Blake. Hadn't he missed a day or two of school last week due to a virus?

Of course, it was the flu. She and Oliver had been careful.

"Hey." Kat's brown eyes were serious. "You okay?"

"I'm fine. Just thinking about Oliver." *And the possibility I could be pregnant.* The thought churned through her stomach. God help her, but what would she do if she was…? *No.* She would not even consider it. How many years had she tried with Stuart and failed? This was simply her out-of-whack periods acting up.

Kat put down her fork. "His death hurt you more than your divorce from Stuart."

"Yeah," Lee admitted.

"That's because Oliver Duvall was your best friend since grade school, Lee. You two had a lot of history."

She did not want to discuss Oliver, or the fact she missed him more than she'd ever missed her ex-husband after their divorce.

No, what she wanted was to discuss Rogan Matteo.

"He makes my fingers tingle." There—it was out in the open. Matteo's effect on her.

"Oliver made your fingers tingle?" Kat curled into the sofa's corner with a cup of tea.

"No…. Argh." Lee rested her head on the back of the couch. "Rogan Matteo. Your guest. Tonight, he introduced himself while I was checking my plane. Apparently, he wants transportation back and forth to the mainland for a couple of weeks."

Kat laughed. "Ah…I see."

"It's not funny," Lee retorted.

"Attractions usually aren't."

"I am *not* attracted to him," Lee said, vexed that her sister had jumped to conclusions.

"Oh, I can see that," Kat said. "Mr. Hunk walks up the pier, pins you with his sorrowful eyes while the wind plays in all that sexy black hair and then he opens his mouth and out comes an accent that would make Matthew McConaughey weep, and your fingers get an irritable little tingle. Yep, you're definitely not attracted."

Lee closed her eyes. "This is the silliest discussion I've had since sixth grade."

"Back at you, sis. But it's good you're attracted, don't you think? After your divorce from the rat B, and then hooking up with poor Oliver, it means—"

"It means Rogan Matteo is a potential fare, Kat. That's all." Lee did not want to think about *poor Oliver* or she'd be crying into her pillow half the night. Nor did she want to think she was dishonoring him eight weeks after his death by eyeing up another man. Jeez, that alone made her nauseous. She was not her mother. *Not.*

"Okay," Kat conceded, "he's a fare. So *are* you flying him?"

"I haven't decided. It's a big responsibility getting someone to work every day."

"Oh, heck," Kat scoffed. "Take the guy. If after a week he's too much of a hassle, tell him to go with Lucien."

Lee sighed. Her sister had a point. She was making

far too much of all this. And just because Matteo had kind eyes.

Like Oliver's.

Oliver. Best friend turned lover weeks ago, while on a six-week furlough from Iraq. Before he returned to war. Before he was killed by sniper fire.

For three years after her divorce, Lee had avoided relationships; tamped down the remotest inclination toward desire. Then Oliver Duvall had returned to Firewood Island, and she'd never been so glad to see her childhood friend. When she thought of his death…

How *could* she look at Rogan Matteo with Oliver not barely gone two months? Rogan Matteo with his quiet eyes.

Was it any wonder he appealed to her? The Southern accent molding his words, or the way he looked at his little boy had nothing to do with her…*lust.* It was those slate-gray eyes, reminders of a friend who was no more.

"All right," she said. "I'll tell him my plans if he shows up on my dock again."

"Why not tell him now? Didn't we just see him through the kitchen window, sitting on the cabin porch, looking at the stars? Go knock on his door."

Lee stared at her sister. "Are you crazy? It's the middle of the night."

Kat raised a brow. "It's ten after nine."

"You *are* crazy."

"Honey, I'm not blind. The guy *is* handsome…in a rough-edged sort of way. If he makes your fingers itch, go talk to him. You know you want to." She grinned. "Look, what's he going to do? Say hi?"

"It'll seem like I'm chasing him."

"Oh, for heaven's sake. Do you want the damn fare or not?"

"Fine." Before she could change her mind, Lee set down her cup, got up and walked out the back door. The way her stomach roiled, a breath of cold air would do her good.

Stepping onto the back deck, she realized she should've grabbed her coat; the night chill crept under her lightweight sweater, goose-bumping her skin. Above, stars cluttered the sky, magnifying its vastness and if she had a moment she'd seek out the Big and Little Dippers, as always. But Rogan had spotted her and was likely wondering about her intentions.

Now or never, Lee.

Starting across Kat's backyard toward the cabin's path in the woods, she watched him rise from the wicker chair and come to the edge of the steps in anticipation of her arrival.

He hadn't turned on his outside light and so stood in the dark, looming above her. Around them, night breezes whispered through the trees, bearing the tang of sea salt.

"It's Lee Tait," she said, hugging her arms around her stomach against the night's chill. Against him.

"Hello, Lee."

God, how could her name sound *that* husky?

"I was visiting my sister and figured I should let you know that flying you to Renton won't be a problem. But before you go jumping up and down with glee, I'll be frank. This is a three-day tryout, Mr. Matteo. After that we'll see where we're at."

A punch of silence, then a low chuckle. "You don't beat around the bush, do you, Captain Tait? I like that."

"Good. We understand each other."

"We do."

"Fine. I'll see you later."

Before she could turn back down the path, he asked, "Ms. O'Brien is your sister?"

"For thirty-four years. Argh—" Lee massaged the spot between her eyes. "She'll kill me if you reveal that detail."

"I'll be sure to tape my mouth shut." Again, she heard a note of humor as he glanced toward the Victorian. And abruptly, a thought hit. Maybe she'd read him wrong. Maybe it wasn't her he was interested in, but Kat.

And why not? a voice whispered. Of the three sisters, Kat was the nurturer, the earth mother. The intermediary Lee and Addie always came to for advice when life's inroads got rough.

"Just for the record," Lee pointed out. "Kat doesn't gossip. Nor would she have convinced me to bother you tonight—" *Now, why tell him that, Lee?* "—except I bugged her with some questions." *Oh, great word choice.*

"About me?" His voice lowered to Vin Diesel deepness.

"For insurance purposes."

"That standard for all your passengers?"

He had her there. "Look," she said, trembling from the cool breeze. "I'll be honest. Your—"

"You're cold," he interrupted, coming down the steps, shrugging from his vest. "Why don't you come inside for a minute?"

Go inside that little cabin? Where his big frame would swallow every molecule of air? Where she'd wander close enough to smell the soap on his skin? No thanks.

Before Lee could think it through, he'd wrapped

the vest, infused with his warmth and scent, around her shoulders.

"I'm fine," she said, back-stepping so they weren't so close, so she couldn't feel his breath on her forehead. "Besides, I need to get back to my sister."

He dropped his hands from the panels of the vest where he'd pulled them closed over her breasts. "I don't bite, Lee," he said softly.

"Maybe not," she replied, hoping to inject some clout into her tone because she wanted nothing more than to grab his face between her hands. "But you have to admit, your nightly vigil down at the docks was downright spooky. What was I to think? No, let me rephrase that. What were *you* thinking? A man with your obvious intelligence and a lawyer to boot should know better than to stand there staring at a woman three nights in a row, especially when she's by herself."

Huffing a breath, he shoved his hands into the pockets of his jeans. "My apologies. You're right. I wasn't thinking. All that mattered, *still* matters, is my son, Ms. Tait. He's my first priority. Everything else falls by the wayside."

"Well." Her irritation faded upon his reference to the child. "At least we have that cleared up." She hesitated. "I understand you bought Eve Riley's old farm and that you're renovating the house." Kat had let that tidbit drop at dinner.

"I did and am." He smiled, a flash of white in the dark. "This for insurance purposes, too?"

"Absolutely," she quipped. "Especially when you don't look like any farmer I know."

She thought he might chuckle, but instead his gaze took in the dark woods behind her. "I'm a defense attorney."

Which meant he litigated for the underdog or the criminal. Yet it didn't explain why he'd relocated his child in the middle of the school term—and on an island—while he continued to work on the mainland, a seemingly unfair decision. More so, where was the boy's mother? *Was* she the second Matteo in the business card's "Matteo and Matteo"?

"Is your wife a lawyer, too?"

His eyes dulled. "No."

"Will she be joining—"

"No."

Lee shivered. The way he said that one word…. "I'm sorry," she said. "It's none of my business."

He stood frozen, quiet—which told her more than she had a right to know. Rogan Matteo was the sole guardian of his son. The reasons weren't important, but they were enough to stay on her guard. Daddy role models were not a favored part of her life. Her father had left Charmaine when Lee was a toddler. Two decades later, her own marriage had dissolved in a raw divorce after her inability to conceive—and her ex's infidelity.

"See you in a week." She spun around.

"Lee, wait. I need you to fly me tomorrow."

"Tomorrow? I thought you were on vacation." Again, according to Kat.

"I am, but I just found out I'll need to be in Renton for a 9:00 a.m. meeting. I can take the afternoon ferry back if you're not available."

She mulled over her options. "Fine. I'm flying my brother-in-law to Renton at one, I can fly you back then. That time frame work for you?"

"Yes, and thank you. See you at eight-fifteen?"

"Till then." She shrugged out of his vest, reluctant to let go of his scent. *Get a grip, Lee.* "Goodbye, Mr. Matteo."

"Rogan," he corrected, taking the garment she shoved into his hand. "And goodnight, Lee."

She hurried down the path, the timbre of his voice lingering in her ear. The prickle in her fingers sharpened.

Tomorrow, she'd fly him over, and afterward find an excuse to boot him off her plane and out of her life.

Determined, she said goodbye to Kat and Blake, and drove home. Two hours later, Rogan Matteo's mellow Southern accent continued to whisper across her skin.

He slept in spurts, getting out of bed when dawn edged a line of pink onto the horizon. Today he would be climbing into a plane with a woman pilot. A woman whose moves attracted him, whose hair framed her face in a way that was sexy as hell.

A woman with whom he'd spend twenty minutes flying across ocean water. *Not a lake and not in the mountains,* he reasoned. *It's not the same geography Sophie and Darby flew over.*

His heart bounced in his chest. Although the radiant heating had clicked on at 5:00 a.m. and the cabin was warming, he felt a chill. Shoving away visions of confined cockpits, he checked on Danny across the hall. Curled in a ball, blankets cocooned around his small body, his son slumbered the sleep of the innocent.

Rogan touched the boy's shoulder, felt its fragility, and a surge of protection blew through him. *I'll always be here for you, son. I won't let you down.*

Leaving the boy to sleep for another couple of hours, he went to shower. Minutes later, he dressed, then headed for the kitchen to pour cereal into a pair of thick, ceramic bowls.

By eight o'clock, briefcase in hand, he locked up the cabin and ushered Danny out to the truck.

"You know that Mrs. Huddleston will be taking you to school this morning, right, buddy?" Rogan stood in the open door of the rear passenger seat and waited for his son to buckle up. He hated the thought of dropping Danny at the old lady's house this one time, but she lived across from the school, and she'd been a caretaker of kids for years. Rogan had done an extensive check in case he needed her assistance when he had to leave before the school's doors opened. As he did today.

Dan's blond hair fell into his eyes.

"Tomorrow we'll get you a haircut," Rogan continued.

"Don't wanna."

"Ah. You want to look like a rock star," he cajoled, hoping to draw a smile from his son as he tugged the collar of the boy's red jacket from the back of his thin neck. Danny had been surly since he crawled from bed an hour ago.

"No-o."

"A shaggy dog then?"

"No. Let's just go, Dad."

Rogan held in a sigh. "Okay, pal." After closing the door, he went around the hood, got behind the wheel, and started the engine. Hoping for a trace of eagerness on his son's face, he glanced in the rearview mirror.

Danny stared out the side window at the cabin, his mouth a line of mutiny.

Okay, then. Driving down the timbered lane of the B

and B to Shore Road, Rogan offered, "Mrs. Huddleston said there's a boy your age she also takes to school. His name's Bobby and he's in your class."

No answer.

"You know I'd stay home if I could, Daniel, but I need to attend this meeting with Uncle Johnny."

Still no response. Checking the mirror again, he felt his heart lurch. A tear clung to his son's cheek. The sight nearly had him pulling to the roadside, except he couldn't afford to miss his flight with Lee Tait, and Danny needed to be on time for school. "Talk to me, buddy," he tried again. "Please."

The boy's bottom lip quivered. He continued to view the ocean through the trees. "I wanna go to my old school."

Translation: *I hate making new friends.*

"And I wanna go home."

The house in Renton. "Aw, bud. This is our home now."

"I don't wanna live here no more."

"Okay, but we'll have to sell Juniper and Pepper."

"No!" Danny's eyes clashed with Rogan's in the mirror. "Can't we take the horses with us?"

"Do you think that's fair? The farm is their home. Besides…" Rogan played another angle, one that garnered a smidgen of guilt. "They're animals. They'll get confused in a new place."

He had turned down Main Street before the boy's reply drifted from the rear seat. "Okay, we can stay. I don't want them to feel lost."

A stone hit Rogan's gut. Danny transposed his own emotions onto the mare and foal. Reaching back, he patted the boy's knee. "Everything's going to work out, buddy. You'll see."

But after he dropped Danny at Mrs. Huddleston's house, the pledge spun like a merry-go-round through his mind as he drove toward Lee Tait's pier.

She was shoving a box into the cargo hold of the seaplane, and the morning sun forged her thick ponytail into coils of copper.

"Good morning," she called when he climbed from his truck.

"'Morning." Pocketing his keys, he remembered how, twelve hours before, she'd appeared out of the night like a forest sprite. *Jeez, Rogan. What the hell's got into you?* He strode down the wooden dock as she lifted a box of packages. "Let me get those."

"Thanks, but I've done this a time or two, Mr. Matteo."

"Not while I've been in the vicinity." Setting down his briefcase, he stepped beside her on the pontoon, and pushed the box onto the plane.

Planting her hands on hips nicely encased in a pair of black slacks, she canted an icy green gaze up at him.

"Okay," she said and the sexy look of those aviator sunglasses perched on her head zapped through his veins. "Let's get one thing straight here and now. I am not a helpless female in need of rescue. I've logged over ten thousand flying hours in fifteen years, and in that time I've transported luggage, snow and ski gear, fishing and hunting gear, vehicle and engine parts, medical supplies, animals in cages—you get the picture?"

Despite his woozy belly at the thought of getting into a plane for the first time since the crash, he chuckled. "Yes, ma'am. You are quite capable of loading your plane. Alone."

"Thank you. Now, why don't you leave your briefcase here with me and climb aboard." She gestured to the cockpit. "We'll be taking off in five minutes."

A lump bounced into his windpipe. The seat appeared narrow, constricted…sized for a ten-year-old. "You want me to…"

"Settle yourself into the co-pilot's chair. Unless you'd rather sit behind me in the passenger seat."

Somehow the thought of her not beside him made his mouth go dry. He needed to see her face, the astuteness in her eyes, the calm she would offer when he no doubt lost it a mile up in the clouds.

A small crease staged itself between her fine auburn brows. Was she assessing him, wondering if she should fly him after all? *Come on. Get in the damn plane before she figures out you're a candy-ass flier.*

With epic effort, he stepped toward the door. His shoes felt bulky as cement, his legs as if they were chained to the dock's planks.

"Rogan." She touched the sleeve of his suit coat. Her eyes held compassion. "Have you flown in a small plane before?"

He swallowed. "Not recently."

Her eyes narrowed. "Is this your first time up?"

"I've flown in commercial jets." Where there were center seats, broad aisles and hundreds of passengers. "I'm fine," he said when her hand dropped away. Biting his tongue, he climbed into the plane, squeezed his big body between the front seats, and landed on the co-pilot's cushioned chair.

The front windshield exposed a propeller, and dual bands of blue: one of sky, the other of ocean. Sweat popped from his pores.

The plane swayed and rocked gently on the water as Lee finished loading her cargo; then she scrambled into the pilot's chair and pulled the door shut.

Her brows knitted. "Need something to settle your stomach?"

"Took it with breakfast."

"Good. Put on the headset," she instructed, back to business. "That way we can talk to each other."

"I'm not much of a conversationalist when I'm in a plane."

He glanced over, tried to smile. She had a modesty he rarely saw in women. A modesty that had nothing to do with her green eyes and kinky ponytail or her freckled hands on the controls, all of which seemed at odds with the white V of blouse between the panels of her black flight jacket. A modesty that went hand-in-hand with her practical demeanor.

The entire package attracted the hell out of him.

She pushed the headset into his hands. "Put it on anyway."

"Do you mind if I close my eyes?" *Yeah.* That's what he'd do. And then he'd contemplate all Lee Tait's assets, including that wild red hair and those slim hips and— The plane's engine roared to life.

"You can do anything you want." Her voice glided along his senses. "Long as you remain buckled, and don't touch the controls."

"Got it." Touching the controls? God forbid. Pinching his eyes shut, he folded his arms, tried not to clutch the fabric of his suit coat.

Perspiration dampened his forehead. His stomach whirled.

Nothing will happen. Danny won't be left behind. But the image of his family wavered behind his eyes.

He tried not to think of what they had gone through when their plane crashed into the mountain forest, breaking branches and small tree trunks, swathing a path of demolition and death.

He tried not to think of his little boy alone in the world, crying for him. Or of Johnny attempting to console Danny. Raising Danny....

"I'm right beside you," Lee said into the headphones when the plane began to move.

He listened to her voice while she ran through a list of checks—rudders, flaps, fuel gage—and gave their coordinates to the Renton tower before the plane skimmed the ocean, lifted, buzzed into the sky.

He heard the tone of her words more than their meaning. That assured tone. The quiet, steady tone.

And when he bit the inside of his cheek, he felt her fingers curve around his forearm. "You'll be okay with me," she promised.

And, in that moment, he believed her. He really did.

Chapter Three

Lee kept her word and landed with barely a bounce on the south end of Lake Washington near Renton's seaplane base. Still, as he climbed out of the craft, Rogan could have bowed to the floating dock, so grateful was he to be earthbound again.

Now, riding the elevator ten floors up to the law offices he and Johnny had established eight years ago, he recalled her piloting skills again. She *had* eased his thundering pulse in the way she handled the plane. With a little luck, he'd take that ease to his brother. After three long, heart-breaking and guilt-ridden years, Rogan had come to hate the mere mention of the charter airline responsible for taking his family, and he suspected this meeting would be more of the same frustrating roller-coaster ride.

When he entered the reception area, the woman at the

desk raised her head. "Mr. Matteo. It's good to see you again, sir." As if he'd been gone ten years rather than ten days. "Your brother is expecting you."

"Thanks." Briefcase in hand, he headed down the hallway leading to the big L-shaped corner office—his old stomping grounds—with its spectacular view of Mount Rainier. When he left, Johnny had claimed the space. At the thought, Rogan expected a twinge of regret and envy. None came.

The door stood open. His brother sat behind the expansive cherrywood desk where Rogan had spent years reviewing cases and interviewing clients. He knocked softly on the doorjamb.

"R.B." A big grin flashed across Johnny's face. "I was wondering if you'd come."

"I almost didn't." He set the briefcase beside the small comfortable sofa, and went to the credenza for some coffee. "Want some?" he asked, tossing a dollop of cream into a mug.

Johnny shook his head. "Already had enough to sink a ship."

Rogan lowered himself to the earth-toned sofa. "What's up?"

Chuckling, Johnny came around the desk to sit in the adjacent chair. "You never were one to waste time."

"Yeah, well, maybe I should have," he muttered, reprimanding himself for the years of work he'd prized, including the day his world collapsed.

Crossing his arms, his brother sat back. "And maybe you should give yourself a break."

Rogan glanced up. "I need you to be a brother, John. Not a frickin' shrink."

Johnny sighed. "All right. Here's the deal. They've upped the ante for an out-of-court settlement."

They would be Abner Air. He hated the name, hated that—to him—it sounded hillbillyish. Most of all, he hated that he had to sue for slack maintenance, which he believed resulted in the crash of the single-prop plane Darby and Sophie boarded.

I don't feel good about this trip, Rogan. Fisting his hands on his thighs, he battled back his dead wife's parting words. Words which could still haunt him deep in the night.

"How much this time?" he asked. His jaw ached.

Johnny quoted the price.

Anger heating his blood, Rogan stood and walked to the windows. Across the city, Rainier rose like a white-crusted jewel. He'd learned to ski on her slopes. "The only reason they want to settle out of court is because they're guilty as sin." Turning, he faced his brother. "They don't want media coverage. But they're going to pay, and it'll be *in* court with the media present. I want them exposed."

A long moment passed. Finally, Johnny said, "I think you should go for the deal, R.B. If we go to trial, you may come away with a helluva lot less. You've worked against big companies. You know the game."

"Cutthroat. I know. But I don't give a rat's ass. These people deserve every damn thing we can throw at them."

Johnny studied him. "Is that why you bailed on Matteo and Matteo? Because you thought we were getting too ruthless?"

"I didn't bail. I wanted something different, with a different outlook." One that offered a slower pace of life, and saw the heart of a client's problems, not the size of his wallet.

"And you'll be paid in peanuts for your effort," Johnny grumbled. "I've done some checking of my own. That island is inhabited by a bunch of hippie offspring."

Rogan thought of Lee, the most structured person he'd met in years. "They're not all loosey-goosey, John," he said in defense of her. "However, that's not the issue here." Spinning on his heel, he paced the length of the windows. "These SOBs are hiding something. I want to know what it is, and I want to know yesterday."

Johnny's eyes were grim—and sad. "We may never know why that plane went down, Ro. Let's take the deal and put an end to this."

Rogan clenched his fists. "There'll never be an end because the other half of my family will never come back."

"Okay. Okay." Elbows to knees, Johnny pushed both hands into his dark hair and gusted a sigh. "I may have a lead on another avenue, anyway. But let me sort through it first."

"Fine. Keep me posted."

"Always." His brother's mouth curved. "Now, tell me, how's life down on the farm?"

Rogan returned to the sofa, stretched his legs. The mere mention of his new property calmed him. "House should be finished by the end of next week."

"Dan's excited?"

"Oh, yeah. We take daily treks to see the foal."

"Still can't believe you're doing this. An *island* for God's sake, never mind a farm."

"It's what Daniel needs." Truth was, he'd checked out

Firewood Island because Sophie had adored the classic story, *Misty of Chincoteague.* Sophie who, after reading the book, had asked at dinner one night, *Can we live on an island, Daddy, and have a pony?* and he'd replied, *Only dreamers live on islands.*

Could he have been any more obtuse to his little girl? Well, *he* would be that dreamer now, be what Sophie had yearned for in the purity of her heart. Most of all, he'd be a father Danny could count on.

"Whatever the case," he went on, thinking of the homey little office he hoped to rent above the coffee shop in Burnt Bend. "We're where we want to be. It's quiet, laid-back, and the people are friendly."

"And you don't have to walk the rooms where they lived," Johnny said quietly.

Rogan closed his eyes. A headache stitched into his temple. "Let it go, all right? Just make Abner Air pay."

"I'll do my best." Abruptly, his brother stood. "Come on. Breakfast's on me."

"Thought you'd never ask."

At the door, Johnny shouldered into a dark designer jacket. "For what it's worth, I'm sorry, R.B."

Words he'd heard a hundred-fold. "Yeah. Me, too."

At one and on her second flight to the mainland that day, Lee again skimmed the seaplane across Lake Washington. A tall, charcoal-suited figure stood on the dock, briefcase in hand, black hair tousled by the breeze.

Rogan.

The sight of him sent a pang into her belly. She wouldn't consider herself an empathetic woman—not like her sisters Addie and Kat whose hearts rode their sleeves most of the time—yet something about Rogan Matteo dug deep.

Standing there as she taxied in he seemed almost forlorn and a little…lost.

"That your fare back?" her brother-in-law asked from the co-pilot's seat. Skip Dalton had married Addie last Thanksgiving, following a thirteen-year separation incited by their fathers because Addie had become pregnant in high school. When Lee thought of the despair her baby sister endured through those years, it made her chest hurt. Thank goodness for Skip's return to Firewood Island. Today, Addie's joy spilled from every glance, word and smile.

Maneuvering the plane gently into the dock's bay, Lee said, "That's him." She wasn't looking forward to another angsty trip, and planned on advising Matteo to use Duvall's foot ferry in the future.

Skip gathered up a battered attaché case from the rear seat. "Yep, looks like an ambulance chaser, all right," he wisecracked.

She unbuckled her safety belt and felt a pang for the man on the pier. "Truth is, lawyer jokes aside," she said, "he's been a decent guy so far."

"Huh. What I can't figure is why he bought a farm." Skip pursed his lips. "Wouldn't surprise me if he plans to put up a string of beach houses."

She glanced out the window. The man stared back at her as though he eavesdropped on their discussion. Surely, he wasn't hoping to rezone the Riley place into a cluster of grandiose properties?

Skip shot her a wicked grin. "Let's ask him. If he says yes, you can dump him in the Sound on the way home."

Lee rolled her eyes. "Oh, that makes so much sense."

At Skip's laughter, she threw open the door and climbed from the plane. For all her huff and puff, she couldn't tear her gaze away from Rogan as he walked toward them. Those big shoulders, that wind-messed hair, those deep-set gray eyes… The man was a walking, talking *GQ* cover.

Her brother-in-law stepped forward to introduce himself. "Skip Dalton. I hear you'll be flying with Lee for a while."

Rogan's gaze flicked to her. "Guess news really does fly."

Eyes narrowing, Skip observed the man waiting to board—and watching Lee. "For the record," her brother-in-law said, "we're a close family." With that, he headed down the dock, whistling.

Lee stared after him. Talk about a testosterone standoff.

"Well," Rogan drawled. "That was enlightening."

She took his briefcase, set it on the seat behind the co-pilot's chair. "Don't mind him. As the only adult male in a family of females, he's a little territorial. Especially now that my youngest sister is seven months pregnant. Why don't you get in and we'll head back?"

When they both settled in the cockpit, she reignited the engine. "You okay?" The color had left his face once more and his hands gripped his knees.

"I'm fine."

He didn't look fine. "Concentrate on my voice." She steered the plane toward open water, went through her checklist. Rudders, flaps, fuel, wind velocity…. "If you're this uncomfortable flying," she advised when she saw him clench his fists, "you should seriously consider traveling by water, regardless of the schedule."

"I won't do that to my son. Schools can be terrifying for the new kid."

Then maybe you shouldn't have moved to our island.

As if their minds were linked, he said, "I don't plan to do this much longer, anyway."

"Oh?" Did he mean lawyering?

"I can't explain—" He released a gut-deep groan as the plane lifted off the water and arrowed into the sky.

Issuing the coordinates to the tower, Lee kept vigil on her passenger. His mouth was a pale, stark line; his eyes focused on his knees jutting in the confines of the cockpit. Single prop planes were not vessels of comfort for a man with a lumberjack's frame. Or, one with an apparent phobia.

"I'll get you home safe," she offered. "Weather's clear. Great day for flying."

Maybe if he talked about the root of his problems, he'd realize planes weren't all bad.

"What happened to you to make you this nervous, Mr. Matteo?"

They were almost across the Sound when he finally pried his tongue loose. "I lost half my family when their plane used a forest as a landing strip."

Ah, geez. "Rogan…" Lee felt sick at heart for what he must have suffered. "I don't know what to say."

For the first time he looked at her. An ocean of pain glimmered in his eyes. "It's been three years and, hell, I don't know what to say. I'm still trying to figure it out, still trying to fix what's left of my family."

Turning away, he focused on his knees again. "All night I kept thinking, What if something goes wrong? What'll happen to my boy? He's seven, just a baby. He needs me to stick around, be there until he can take care of himself. I also know the probability of dying in a car crash exceeds that of dying in a plane, and that my apprehension is all out of whack. But there you have it."

Except he *had* experienced tragedy-by-plane. "I'm so sorry."

He blew a long sigh, scraped at his hair. "Hell, it's me who should be sorry, dumping on you like this."

"No," she said. "You have a right to feel the way you do." And she meant it. Losing half a family… She shook her head, unable to imagine the horror, the grief.

"A defective fuel line is what they're claiming," he went on. "More like poor maintenance on the part of Abner Air."

Abner Air? *Oh. My. God.* He'd lost his family in *that* plane?

Now it all came to her, the niggle in the back of her mind when he'd said his name. *Matteo.* Four months after she walked out of her marriage and Stuart's company, news about her ex's plane going down had filtered back to Lee.

She had recognized the pilot's name, Bill Norton. But the names of the passengers had been unfamiliar…*forgotten.*

Yes, she'd sympathized from afar but by then, Stuart Hershel was already someone else's husband—and an almost daddy. Because of the latter, because of the way she'd discovered Stuart's betrayal, Lee had put the past, including the crash, wholly out of her mind.

Now she remembered snippets. A woman and child—with Rogan's last name.

His family.

"Look," he said, unaware her heart struggled like a

wounded animal. "Can we start over?" This time his gaze was soft and gray as the morning mist.

With a nod, Lee forced her throat to open. "Sure." For two elongated seconds their eyes held, and her heart emitted a solid thump against her breastbone. Start something with this man? *No and no.*

Quickly turning her concentration on navigating her seaplane—previously of Stuart's fleet, *oh, God*—she forwarded her status to the tower and began reducing her elevation.

Minutes later, she taxied shoreward to her portion of pier extending from Burnt Bend's boardwalk.

She couldn't wait to leave again, make the run to pick up Skip. Anything to get away from Rogan and the pain she now knew hovered behind his eyes.

While she tied the plane to the wooden deck, he stood facing the shoreline meandering westward. A forest of hemlocks, cedars and willows traveled the land's slope to the water, but Lee knew what lay on the other side of the natural buffer a mile from town. The Riley property, now his land.

He slanted a look over his shoulder toward the boardwalk's shops and restaurants. "I hope to buy some office space there."

A lawyer in Burnt Bend? Except… What had he said before takeoff? *I don't plan to do this for long.*

"Are you changing careers?" she asked.

Again he viewed the trees hiding his future address. "In a way."

A crooked smile that displayed one front tooth edging a millimeter below its twin, stalled her breath. The man didn't know his own potency.

She had to avoid him. At all costs. Her past meshed too closely with his.

"Same time next week?" he asked.

Make a decision, Lee. Her mouth refused to open. Grateful she hadn't removed her aviators—she was certain he'd be able to read her misgivings—she nodded once. "Right."

With a clip of his head, he started for his blue truck, parked in the graveled lot nearby. Not until his dark-suited form disappeared from sight did she grab the wingtip of her plane to support her shaky legs.

Half his family had died in a tragedy that might have been averted had she not been so focused on saving her splintering marriage.

Two days later, Lee lay on an examination table in a Seattle medical clinic, still worrying over her link to Rogan Matteo, a link of which he was unaware, but that she understood clearly.

Why hadn't she followed her gut instincts three years ago? Why had she trusted her ex to inform the authorities. *Why, why, why?*

Her worry knotted her throat and propelled her nausea—until she was forced to seek out her friend Dr. Lily Ramirez. Just to talk, Lee told herself. Lily would know what to do. Because a hundred years ago, she'd been Lee and Oliver's classmate and, later, as an ob-gyn, Lily had seen Lee through a horde of fertility tests during Lee's nine-year marriage to Stuart.

Staring at the ceiling, Lee shivered at a thought. Was it worry causing the nausea or was it something else?

Once, years ago, she had experienced similar

symptoms; periodic queasiness after the evening meal, a craving for raspberry jam and the distaste of her beloved morning coffee.

She couldn't be pregnant. It had to be the stress of the past two days.

But the longer she waited for Lily to arrive, the more Lee questioned the possibility. The first sign of nausea had begun two weeks before Rogan's disclosure.

The door opened and Lily entered. "Hey, friend." The doctor's lips curved in a genuine smile.

"Lily," Lee greeted her, relieved. "Am I glad to see you."

The doctor scanned the nurse's information on the file she held. "You've been nauseous for a couple of weeks?"

"I might be in trouble—big trouble."

"Okay, don't panic." Lily took Lee's hand. "Tell me."

Lee did. She explained the wooziness and her worries.

"First," Lily said after Lee quieted, "let's see if you are pregnant. Then we'll talk."

Several minutes later, the internal exam completed, the doctor removed her gloves. "Your uterus is slightly swollen, but we'll do a blood and urine test to verify." Tossing the soiled toweling into the trash, she asked, "Do you have an idea of when you might have gotten pregnant?"

"February. The night before Oliver Duvall shipped out, a little over eight weeks ago." *For the last time.* The paper pillow rustled as she turned her head. "But we were careful."

"Doesn't matter how careful you are," Lily replied gently, washing her hands in the sink. "Accidents happen, Lee. I'll get the nurse in for the tests, then we'll talk." She left the room, the door whooshing closed behind her.

Lee stared at the counter with its sink and shelves and medical supplies, at the stirrups protruding from the end of the table. Could things get any worse?

And dare she hope? Dare she hope for a baby after all the barren years?

Ten minutes later, dressed again, she sat on the exam bed and observed Lily jot notes on her clipboard. "Well?" Lee asked, her heart pounding.

"You are pregnant."

Lee closed her eyes. What a mess. What a wonderful, scary, couldn't-come-at-a worse-time mess.

She was having Oliver's baby. Oliver, a man she'd known and trusted since forever. A man who had made soldiering his life—until it killed him.

Gazing at the woman, whose fuchsia-colored stethoscope draped her neck like a trendy piece of bling, Lee's mind whirled with future scenarios. The baby's health, due to Lee's age. The birth process, another health worry. Her fledgling company. No question, she'd have to sell Sky Dash. A single mother operating a plane *and* raising a baby? Impossible feat.

"God, I can't believe this happened, Lily. You know my periods are always so unpredictable, and since the divorce I didn't bother with the pill. What was the point of regulating them, right? And, in case you're wondering, he wasn't blasé and I wasn't stupid. We used condoms."

"Condoms can tear," Lily said gently.

Lee stared at the floor. "It wasn't supposed to happen," she whispered. "You know how close we were as kids, right? You, me, him. Best friends forever. But on this furlough…"

"Things changed," Lily filled in.

"Yeah." Lee remembered Oliver's face that last day. She'd flown him to the naval air base on Whidbey Island, where they'd held each other for an eternity. She realized then that walking away from her marriage to Stuart had been a relief; but walking away from her lifelong friend had put a dent in her heart.

A tear slid down her cheek. "I want this baby to live, Lil."

"First and foremost—no stress. And no negative thoughts." The doctor's hand gripped Lee's. "Do what you have to do because this may be your last chance. You're thirty-seven, Lee. And that means—"

"I know, I know. My eggs are petrifying."

Lily chuckled. "Well, not quite."

"But close. Funny, isn't it? Stuart and I tried for eight years and when it finally happened I miscarried after the first month. Oliver and I do it once, and…" Abashment warmed her skin. Lord. She didn't know whether to hope, pray or wish. "Do you think it'll make a difference because it's his?"

Lily dabbed Lee's tears with a tissue. "I can't answer that. However, I can outline a strict and careful routine for you. I'll also prescribe an antinausea medication. Don't worry," she said with a smile. "It's been on the market for years, for just these conditions."

"That's good, because I still have a plane to fly."

"Today it moves into second place," Lily said firmly. "From this point on, baby comes first."

If he lived. *Yes,* Lee thought, hoping. *It's a boy.* With

Oliver's smile, Oliver's eyes. Eyes that offered the same gentleness she recognized the night Rogan Matteo had chased the cold away with his warm vest.

Oh, Lee. How much worse can it get? Here you are, pregnant with the baby of one man while lusting after another.

Who would've guessed that she, still a virgin on her twenty-third birthday, would shuffle through men quick as a cardplayer fourteen years later?

At nine o'clock Friday morning, Rogan stood on the boardwalk facing a narrow door that led up to the apartment above Coffee Sense, a shop that brewed some of the best java he'd tasted in a long while. Last weekend, when he noticed the For Rent sign in the upstairs window, he had immediately called the number listed. Apparently, the owners of the coffee shop and its top floor recently lost their tenant to Bremerton and they'd needed another lessee. After a quick tour, Rogan signed the agreement.

Jingling the keys in his hand, he looked toward the cove. The boardwalk arced in a horseshoe at the conclusion of Main Street. The right annex of the shoe consisted of ferry docks, a few craft shops and a seafood pub; the left extension hosted several local clothing stores, the Tuscany Grill, Art Smarts, Coffee Sense—and Lee's pier.

He admired the quaint maritime architecture of each building: wood siding in a variety of bold colors, weathered cabled roofs, storefronts circa 1930 with scripted or printed signs.

Most of all, he liked that Coffee Sense was the last shop on the boardwalk's left curve—and a few dozen yards from where Lee moored her seaplane. That detail had him smiling as he surveyed the spot where, within the hour, her red-and-white Cessna would once again rock lazily on the sun-dappled water.

After signing the lease yesterday, he'd stood with Danny at the upstairs window and watched Lee lift easily into the air on her afternoon mail run.

"There's the lady's plane," his son pointed out. *"Are you gonna see her all the time?"*

An innocent question with conflicting connotations. Yes, in a sense, he would see her "all the time" but not for the reasons he craved, like the heart he believed hidden behind her quick tongue and clever mind. And then there were those flashing green eyes. Reasons that were all about Lee Tait, the woman— *Jeez, Rogan. Forget it already.*

Inserting the key, he unlocked the door and took the steep, narrow stairs to the four-by-four landing where a pair of doors faced each other. With a squeak, the one on the right swung open and he stepped into his new office. The hardwood floors creaked beneath his boat shoes and the musty scent of wood and age filled his nostrils. Yesterday there had been a sense of rightness about the place, which he felt again today as he reassessed the main room, the side kitchen, the five-foot hallway branching into a washroom, bedroom—or second office space—and the rear entry to an outside stairway.

Guilt poked Rogan at leaving the firm he and Johnny had founded. But he couldn't do that life anymore, couldn't live in the house he'd bought with Darby. All he wanted was to live in the new farmhouse, and work Monday to Friday under his own shingle here on the island. Although he'd agreed to work as a quasi-satellite office to the main branch in Renton for special cases, the idea of small town lawyering and taking on garden variety cases appealed to Rogan as nothing had since he'd graduated from Princeton.

Today, his goal was to set up his laptop, shop for some furniture, and prepare to open for business next week.

A droning sound drew him to the front window. Between the slats of the wooden blind a flash of red caught his eye as a seaplane banked left into the cove, the sun sparking off a wingtip. Lee, returning from her morning run.

He appreciated the ease with which she lowered the aircraft, sailed onto the water's surface, steered to the wharf. She was good, very good, at her job. He imagined her voice to the Renton tower. Soft and a little raspy, that voice had calmed his nerves; assured him Danny wouldn't be orphaned.

Suddenly, he wanted to go down and greet her. He wanted to hear her voice again.

He remained where he was, watching through the slats while she removed her headgear, climbed from her plane, anchored it to the dock. His eyes narrowed when a dark-haired man in jeans and plaid shirt approached the craft. Friend? Lover?

A spark of jealousy flared as he watched the guy unload a box from the bantam-size cargo hold behind the passenger seats.

Rogan grunted. What the hell was the matter with him? He wasn't interested in the woman. Damn it, he was not.

Yet, he couldn't tear himself away from the window. A love-struck idiot, he stood watching while she fiddled with her plane and finally headed down the dock toward the coffee shop.

Man, she was something. The way she carried herself. Those long legs. That blazing, curly hair the cove's wind hauled over one shoulder. She wore the same black flight jacket as before, but today her slacks were gray.

Rogan stepped back. He felt like a peeping Tom. *Get your mind back to this office, man.*

On the kitchen counter his laptop waited. Okay, he'd tap out a supply list.

Fifteen items filled the screen when he heard footsteps on the front entry stairs. Wondering about his first visitor, or his neighbor across the landing, he lifted his head toward the door that he had absently left ajar.

Lee poked her head inside.

They stared at each other. Her auburn brows slammed together before she blinked and sauntered into the room.

"What are you doing here?" she asked.

"I've rented the place." Pleasure rushed through him. "What are *you* doing here?"

She gestured to the door. "Guess we're neighbors."

"You have an office across the way?" Could things get any better?

A smile flickered. "I suppose part is office—if you could call it that. Mostly it's my home."

She *lived* next door? His body tightened. He'd see her daily. If he wanted to. And, God help him, but he did. Very much.

She turned in a small circle, viewing the hollow rooms. "Are you planning to be the village's first lawyer?"

His mouth twitched. "Is that better than being the village's first idiot?"

She chortled. "Hey, if the shoe fits." A rosy hue touched her cheeks. "Sorry, scratch that. Sometimes I run off at the mouth."

He tucked his hands into his pockets. "I like pilots who run off at the mouth." *Especially pretty ones like yours.*

"You wouldn't be referring to my rambling during our time in the air the other day, would you? Because all I wanted was to keep you from jumping out the door at five thousand feet."

He rubbed the back of his neck. "And you did a fine job, Captain Tait. I arrived home in one piece, which made my son immensely happy."

Those keen eyes sobered. She looked away.

"What?" he asked, sensing a subtle change in her demeanor.

She shook her head, glanced at the window. "I should be going."

"You were thinking about what I told you. About my family."

She didn't answer. She didn't need to. He knew the information was in her mind. And she pitied him.

"I don't need your emotional charity, Lee," he said. "Or anyone else's. That's not why I moved here."

"Why did you move?" she asked softly.

"To make a new life." And then he understood. "Ah. You think I came to escape."

"What I think is moot. We all have our reasons and means for escaping the ugliness of life. Is yours better or worse than mine?" A shrug. "Look, I have to get some paperwork done." With a small smile, she held up a clipboard he had missed. "See you around."

She was out the door before he could move.

"Wait."

Key in her door, she shoved it open. "You don't need to explain, Mr. Matteo. Your life is your business and I have a habit of intruding."

He shook his head. They were on the tiniest stairwell landing in existence. Emanating from her hair was a blend of sea, sunshine and strawberry shampoo. And those golden freckles on her cheeks… His fingers flexed at his sides, craving a simple touch.

"First," he rasped, voice alien to his ears. "It's Rogan. Second… You're right. About everything."

Her gaze hung on his. Her lips parted with a soft breath.

He wanted to kiss her, more than he'd wanted to kiss a woman in a long, long while. His head bowed, moved in the direction of her mouth. He could hear the hitch of her breath, feel it strike his chin. A current arced between them, hot and searing and electrifying.

"Rogan," she murmured. "No." The word came as softly as the hand she laid against the pocket of his shirt, where his heart thrummed. "This is wrong."

"Wrong?" The heat of her singed his lips.

With a slow headshake, she edged back. "We've barely met and…I'm not looking for someone right now."

Right now. Did that mean she'd be receptive later? The question whirled in his mind as he studied her features. She had the most beautiful eyes. Wide and dark-lashed, which seemed incongruous to her fair coloring. Upon closer examination, he realized black rings circled her irises, tiny barricades defending green gems.

Lifting a hand, he touched a nest of freckles on her cheek.

Her throat worked. "I need to prepare for my next flight," she said hoarsely. And then she was gone, inside her apartment, and he was staring at the peephole in her door.

Chapter Four

Lee leaned against the door and worked to measure her breathing.

He'd nearly kissed her. She nearly let him.

What was she thinking? She was pregnant, for God's sake! With another man's child, a man she honored and loved as a friend. Okay, on that last night the friendship had transferred into a "with benefits" situation, but they'd also talked about marriage. Afterward.

Oliver had asked if she would ever consider tying the knot again and she'd told him only with the right man.

Not that Stuart hadn't been the man. He had—until her inability to conceive or bear a child erected a barrier between them. Until the misery in Stuart's eyes caught the attention of another woman, a woman he'd married immediately after his divorce from Lee, and who had given him a child seven months later.

So much for true love.

And then there was Oliver.

How could she have even considered kissing Rogan?

Yet, her imagination bloomed with his taste, texture, heat and an involuntary tingle ran up her thighs.

Stop it! He's a road to nowhere. One she was determined to avoid. Never mind that he had issues, linking her to her ex-husband in the worst possible way: pilot error. A fact she'd suspected for years, suspected deep in her core.

On a slow inhalation, she let another truth seep in, let herself adapt to the realization that he would be her neighbor. *The man across the hall.*

Fourteen days ago the renter had been a woman, a reclusive environmental artist. Two years and Lee could not remember hearing a sound next door.

Intuitively, Lee knew Rogan would make himself very accessible in the office two steps from her threshold.

Palms to her burning cheeks, she walked across the diminutive apartment, her shoes quiet on hardwood that undulated with the season's temperatures. She would make some tea. Peppermint, to ease her stomach.

A knock sounded on her door. Rogan?

Looking through her peephole Lee saw the distorted face of Lucien Duvall, Oliver's father.

Surprise had her blinking. What did *he* want? The man rarely spoke to her. Even during childhood when she'd played with Oliver, Lily and their friends, he had avoided her.

She didn't need a rocket scientist to explain the senior

Duvall's feelings toward her, and figuring out why had long since grown wearisome. She didn't understand his reasons, she didn't understand him. Still, she had no intention of opening herself up to ridicule. Growing up, she had heard enough ridicule about her mother.

Straightening her shoulders, she swung the door open.

Large and bulky in a navy storm coat, Lucien glared at her with pale blue eyes from the stairwell's muted light. *Like ice,* she thought.

"Lucien."

His hand jerked up and she took a backward step. "I found this," he said. "I think it's yours."

Lee dropped her gaze to his broad, work-hardened fist. A fist strangling a pink silk scarf. She had looked everywhere for the dainty accessory. Between Lucien's thick fingers the fabric looked wispy as smoke.

"Thank you." She took the wrinkled scarf. "Where—"

"In my son's truck. The glove compartment."

"Oh." Then she remembered. Remembered the night Oliver had taken her for a drive to the other side of the island. The night before he had gone back to Iraq. She had worn a belted green shirtdress and arranged the scarf above her collar. When talking transferred to kissing, Oliver had removed the scarf, inhaled its scent, her scent, and stored it in the glove compartment. *I want to take it with me,* he'd told her. *I want something of you there.*

That he'd forgotten the scarf sent a fierce pang through Lee.

"Only one reason your clothes were in his car," Lucien growled.

"What?" Lee blinked.

"You heard me. You've wanted to get your hooks into my son since you was a kid."

"Lucien—"

"Don't think I was blind to what you were up to, Missy."

Lee squared her shoulders. "We were adults." She glanced at the door behind him, Rogan's door—which her neighbor had yet to close completely. Was he listening on the other side?

The old man's eyes grew frigid. "Don't know what Oliver ever saw in you."

She tried to laugh. "To be honest, neither do I. But he was a wonderful friend. I'll always miss him."

He jerked as if slapped. "You're not good enough to miss him."

Before she could acknowledge the cruel remark, her neighbor's door swung wider and Rogan stepped to the threshold. "Trouble?" he asked mildly.

Lucien gave Lee a slit-eyed look, then thundered down the stairs and slammed out the ground-level door.

Lee whistled a breath. "Welcome to Burnt Bend." Vying for a lightheartedness she didn't feel, she asked, "Sure you still want to live and work in our community?"

Rogan set a gentle hand against her cheek. "Wouldn't dream of going anywhere else."

"Then you're braver than most." She turned into her apartment, turned from his touch, the one that had her wanting to press herself into the protection of his big, sturdy chest.

He followed her across the landing and into her doorway. "Lee, who is he to you?"

"Nobody." *Just the grandfather of my baby.* A man who would likely hate her forever when she gave him the news. She tossed the scarf carelessly beside the telephone.

"I don't like his attitude."

She walked to the teapot that continued to steam on the counter. "He has a right to an attitude. He lost a son two months ago in Iraq."

Rogan closed the door and walked into her kitchen. "I can empathize," he said quietly. "Still doesn't give him the right to intimidate you."

"He didn't intimidate me." From the curio, she selected the ten-inch-tall Limoges teapot, her favorite in her heritage collection. "Would you like a cup of peppermint tea?"

"Sure." He moved closer. "This is serious business, Lee. Don't make light of it. I defend victims against people like him."

"I'm *not* a victim, Rogan. You know nothing about me. I was born and raised here. I know these people, know where they've come from, where they've gone. I know their grandmothers and great grandmothers. I know who stole from whom, who screwed whom figuratively and literally, who went to jail, who hates broccoli and who made the Fire High cheerleaders because she had the longest legs and knew how to display them." She took a breath. "It's a small island. I know Lucien Duvall."

"Then why are you shaking?"

"I'm not." Rather than admit he was right, that Lucien had gotten to her, she forced her hands to steady and held out a teacup and saucer. "Look, if I need a lawyer I know where to get one." She attempted a grin and failed. "Would you like a snack? I made a banana-nut loaf yesterday."

His fingers grazed hers as he took the teacup. The familiar gentleness entered his eyes. "Couldn't pass up anything homemade."

She busied herself preparing two slices, cutting him a thicker portion, aware he stood five steps away, aware how much his height and size shrunk her common space.

"Who's Oliver?" Rogan asked.

Lee paused. So he *had* heard the exchange on the landing. "Do you always eavesdrop on people's conversations?" she replied irritably.

"I didn't eavesdrop. At least not until he raised his voice."

Lee relaxed. Only in the last few seconds, as he spoke Oliver's name, had Lucien nearly vibrated with anger. Her heart softened. She, too, had raged when Oliver died.

Rogan set his teacup on the counter and she handed over the plate, and watched him bite into the banana bread with an "mmm" of pleasure at the taste.

"Oliver was a close friend," she said. Her throat squeezed at the void his death left, not just in her life, but in Lucien's who lost his only child.

"How close?"

Her eyes shot to his. "Close, okay?"

"Sorry." He looked at the scarf, its gossamer fabric partially concealing the telephone. "Don't know why I asked. The past isn't… Look, forget it."

She wished she could. "Apology accepted."

With a nod, he set the empty plate on the counter beside his untouched tea. "Thanks for the snack, Lee. It was delicious."

"Would you like some for your son?" she asked before she could think through how her offer would appear to a man who had almost kissed her thirty minutes ago. Who, fifteen minutes ago, had touched her cheek and left a brand she felt still. Whose presence ate the air in the room.

For the first time since he entered her apartment, his mouth curved. "That'd be great. Danny loves bananas."

Moments later, she saw him to the door, the remainder of the loaf wrapped in foil and stored in a plastic container.

"I'll get this back to you tomorrow," he said, nodding to the container.

"Keep it. I have a drawer full."

He paused on the threshold. "Lee, if there's anything you need—"

"I know where you'll be." She pushed him gently onto the landing, the muscles under his shirt strong and warm and inviting. Her hand jerked away. "Let me know if Danny likes the treat." And then she closed the door and flipped the lock.

What was she thinking? If Danny did like the treat, would she bake him another?

Yes, of course, she would.

Staring at the chinaware Rogan had used, she placed a hand against the tiny mound of her stomach. How could she not bake for a child if he asked? Wasn't that part of motherhood?

Except at this stage she wasn't really a mother. Was she? She didn't feel motherly. She felt…tired.

And irritable. Because, God forbid, anything could happen in the next seven months. Well, standing here whining about it wasn't getting her anywhere.

In the kitchen she began rinsing the dishes. No stress,

Lily had said. *Right,* Lee thought. Maybe she ought to call the good doctor, tell her about the baby's grandfather inferring Lee was a slut, and the man across the hall looking at her as if he wanted to get in her pants.

Heck, in comparison, fitting Sky Dash into her life—and her expanding midriff—between now and her due date in October would be a cakewalk.

At seven the next morning she headed for the shoreline trail for her regular Saturday walk with her sisters. With the advance of Addie's pregnancy, their pace had changed from running to brisk walks. Still, she loved these exercise sessions with her sisters. After returning to Firewood Island, she felt closer to Kat and Addie than she ever had in their childhood.

Today, fog whispered over the trees and across the tiny cove, bringing with it dew drops that clung to every surface in sight: budding leaves, blades of grass, stones, pylons and the pier.

Dressed in black yoga pants and a rose-colored sweatshirt, Lee headed for the mouth of the shore trail near her plane. Ahead, the fuzzy gray shapes of her sisters stood waiting.

After hanging her head over the toilet bowl thirty minutes before—she'd forgotten to take her meds—she hoped the cool morning air and the ginger ale in her water bottle would settle her stomach.

"Sorry, I'm late," she said, starting up the path at a steady pace. "How are you feeling this morning, sis?" she asked Addie.

Her younger sister grunted. "Like I've been pregnant forever."

"Not forever." Kat fell in step on Addie's other side. "Just nine more weeks."

"Well," Addie grumbled. "Feels like eternity. All I have to do is look at Skip and I get pregnant."

Lee chuckled. "You're just a highly fertile woman around him."

"And so damned horny it's not even funny."

Kat burst out laughing. "Oh, honey. That was so me when I carried Blake."

"It was?" Lee asked, surprised.

"Really?" Addie chimed in.

"Oh, yeah. I was climbing into Shaun's lap every chance I got. Poor man was exhausted by the time Blake arrived on the scene."

"I would've never guessed," Lee said. "If I recall, you were such a demure little homemaker back then."

Kat snickered. "Well, you know what they say? What goes on behind closed doors and all."

A pensive lull fell as they walked on, the trail spongy with pine needles beneath their feet.

Finally Addie said, "When I was pregnant with Becky I'd cry myself to sleep sometimes because I wanted Skip so bad."

"Oh, Ads." Lee set an arm around her sister's shoulder and hugged her close. Kat wrapped an arm around Addie's waist and, for a short distance there was only the hush of the forest and their soft tread on the trail. Lee imagined they were all remembering Addie in high school—pregnant—and Skip off playing in the NFL. Little did anyone know it was Addie's father and Skip's who'd worked to break the bond between the teenagers, who had their daughter Becky adopted. To this day, the memory still put Lee's pulse rate in an uproar.

It was pure luck, she thought now, *that Skip found Becky, and now he and Addie have the life they've always wanted.*

"Well, then," Kat said finally. "So much for our sex lives—what's new on the Rogan Matteo scene, Lee?"

"Who's Rogan Matteo?" Addie wanted to know.

Lee scowled at Kat. "Just a guy I'm flying to the mainland for a few days," she said, feigning indifference.

"Oh, the one Skip met last Monday at the Renton seaplane dock?" Addie asked.

"Lee has the hots for him."

"Kat," Lee exclaimed. "Will you stop? Next you'll have me marrying the guy."

Her sister's eyebrows bounced. "Now there's an idea."

"Oh, for crying out loud."

"Hey, the man's educated, he's got a solid career *and* a son, who—you have to admit—gives Rogan Matteo a huge edge on responsibility. On top of that, he's pretty darn easy on the eyes."

"Whoa," Lee protested. "If he's so great, why aren't you trying to catch him? He is renting a cabin fifty steps from your back door."

"Because he's not my type. If you recall, I like the brawny blue-collar type. Besides, he's moving into the old Riley place today. And you found him first."

Lee felt her heart kick. In twenty minutes the trail would wind past the ocean side of the Riley property. "You're talking as if I found some hidden treasure," Lee grumbled. "And have you forgotten? Your husband was hardly blue-collar. He had a degree in marine biology."

"A degree he never used," Kat pointed out quietly.

They walked without speaking for several moments, remembering the day four years ago when Kat's husband drowned after a storm swept him off his fishing trawler.

"Anyway," Kat continued. "That's all in the past. As to Rogan, I'll rephrase. He found *you.* And who's to say he isn't a treasure, right, Addie? If Lee likes him, she should go for it."

"Agreed," Addie said. "You need a bit of fun, Lee. All you ever do these days is work on that plane."

"I have bills to pay," she protested, wishing they would get off her case. "Just like you, Kat."

"I also have a child who's asthmatic. That tends to scare off a lot of guys."

Before she could think it through or analyze the consequences, Lee muttered, "So do pregnant, unmarried women."

A songbird trilled in a nearby tree, and somewhere beyond, a squirrel scolded.

Addie cast Lee a look. "What's that supposed to mean?"

She exhaled a shaky breath. "I'm pregnant…and it's Oliver's."

"Omigod, honey." Kat, always the soother, stroked Lee's hair. "When? How?"

"Last time he was home." Her smile wobbled. "And, in the usual way."

"But, you were always just friends…"

"This time it changed," Lee explained "Don't ask why or how. It just…did."

They reached a bend in the fog-patched trail leading past the weathered fence that enclosed the small pasture comprising the Riley farm. *Rogan's farm now,* Lee thought, breathing the briny ocean air sifting through the shoreline trees. Rogan, who had asked about Oliver yesterday and wanted to protect her against Lucien.

"Please," she said. "Do not tell Mom. I couldn't handle her yammering about how I should've taken more care, and how I'm old enough to know better, yada, yada." The last thing she needed was Charmaine ranting as she'd done with Addie fourteen years ago. "I will tell her," Lee continued. "Just not yet, okay?"

Addie hooked their arms. "Got it. We won't say a thing. How are you feeling physically?"

"Woozy this morning because I forgot to take my meds." Lee explained Wednesday's session at the Renton medical clinic, how amazed she'd been after years of trying, after years of irregular menses. "I don't want to lose this baby," she whispered.

"We're here, honey," Addie said. "Every step of the way."

They continued along the wooded path. Above the trees the morning sun struggled to poke beyond the haze; slowly Lee's fear subsided. Kat and Addie *would* be there.

Breathing deeply, she let her mind relax. Beyond the band of evergreens to the right, sea flirted with shore. The constant resonance induced an abrupt rush of love in Lee for her sisters. Here on the island, they had grown up, then separated after high school to begin other lives, endured heartaches, but always stood at each other's backs. It couldn't get any better than this.

She was about to say as much when Addie cried out.

"Addie!" Lee rushed to hold her sister. "What is it?"

"Is it the baby?" Kat asked, clutching Addie's waist.

"No, a—cramp in my leg."

"You need to sit down," Lee said.

Gently, they lowered Addie to the soft, cool earth.

Lee removed her sister's gym shoe. "I'm going to push the ball of your foot upward very slowly," she said. "It'll help unclench the calf muscle. Try to move your foot with me, okay?"

Addie groaned. "Glad one of us got some first-aid training."

Lee maneuvered the foot carefully until Addie's features were no longer pinched and she opened her eyes with a relieved breath. "Thanks," she whispered.

Once they had Addie standing again, Lee said, "I'll call Skip."

"Don't be silly," Addie said. "I'll be okay." But she winced when she set her foot down and attempted to gain her balance.

Lee scowled. "Never mind. I'll call him." But when she tried, the call wouldn't connect. "I'm walking back to where I can get through."

"What about Rogan's place?" Kat suggested. "He's probably got his land line hooked up already."

Lee looked back down the trail they had traveled, back to where it ran alongside his property. Skip would be able to fetch Addie there easier than if he walked a mile through the woods.

"Go," Kat said. "Rogan won't mind."

Of course he wouldn't mind if she used his telephone. In the ten days she'd come to know Rogan Matteo, she had discovered he was a man with principles and decency. A man she could fall for—if she wasn't careful.

Right. Judging by the last two men she'd fallen for, she held the track record for finishing last.

With Rogan… The fact she'd flown for Abner Air and might have been partly responsible for what happened to his family were reasons enough to put her clear out of the running.

Still, she broke into a run down the path toward his property with irrepressible hope in her heart. Raced when she should be turning in the opposite direction, away from him and this silly eagerness rushing through her veins.

Think of Addie, only Addie.

However, when she stood in the pasture, in view of his house and his vehicle, her heart pounded not for her sister but for the man who, if he knew the truth about her, would never speak to her again.

Chapter Five

Rogan watched her climb the pasture fence. *Well, now.*

Mouth twitching, he stacked the clothes box from his truck onto the reconstructed front porch and wondered what Miss Lee was up to today. Oh, yes, he knew the woman walking across the rise of the meadow was his pilot. He'd recognize that curly red ponytail at any distance, even one layered in several hundred yards of fog.

Poking his head into the open door of the house, he called in to his son. "Dan, you going to be all right here for a minute? I need to check on something in the pasture."

"Wait, Daddy," the boy yelled back and Rogan heard small feet on the second floor beating a path to the top of the stairs. "I wanna come with you."

"I'm not going to see Juniper and Pepper." He wished his son were a bit more independent, that it wasn't unease driving him to cling. "It's just Ms. Tait, buddy. Seems she's come to visit."

The boy ran across the living room and, typical seven-year-old, slid to a halt on the hardwood in front of Rogan.

"You know," he said, "you could finish fixing your room, show it to Ms. Tait when you're done."

"Uh-uh. I want to see her, too."

In other words, *I don't want to stay in this scary old house alone.* Not that the house contained ghosts of former owners. No, Danny's ghost was his own anxiety, anxiety that had settled in hard and fast following the deaths of his mother and sister. Thankfully, the island's school counselor understood the trauma and behaviors of her charges. Better, Rogan believed, than the overworked therapist at his son's previous school in Renton.

Danny walked out of the house, tripped down the porch steps, then ran ahead to swing open the gate by the small barn fronting the meadow where the mare and foal were pastured.

Momentarily lost in thoughts of his son, Rogan followed.

The horses were almost invisible in a far corner of their ten-acre domain. Lee, on the other hand, stood in its center, facing the woods and the walking trail, cell phone pressed to her ear.

Danny's hand slipped into Rogan's. "Why's she standing there, Dad? Doesn't she know we're here?"

"Guess not." He observed the tension in her body, the stiffness of her shoulders. Her hand clasped the back of her neck and she bent her head, attentive to her listener.

Rogan slowed his stride, allowing Lee privacy to

complete the call. After she shut the mobile, he called out softly.

She spun around. "Rogan."

The timbre of her voice, that voice haunting his daydreams as well as those in the night, almost had him sprinting for the hills. If her voice could put his pulse in a state of flux, what would happen if he ever kissed her? The last time he'd tried, the heat between them had been palpable.

"Something wrong?" he asked.

"I was coming to use your landline because my sister Addie has a leg cramp. But—" she held up her cell phone "—I was able to get through to her husband after all."

Skip Dalton, the man Rogan met at the seaplane base in Renton.

"Addie's the pregnant one?"

"Yes. She's in a lot of pain and can barely stand."

Rogan put a hand on his son's shoulder. "Danny, I want you to go back to the house, get a few washcloths from the box by the foot of the stairs, then fill the kitchen sink with hot water—hot as you can touch—okay?"

Danny shook his head hard. "I don't wanna go back there." *Alone.*

"Dan, there's a lady who's hurt. I need you to be a brave boy now, okay? I'll be right back, but first I have to see what I can do for Mrs. Dalton."

"But, Dad—"

"It's okay, Rogan," Lee interjected. "I'll see to my sister. If you could point Skip in this direction when he arrives…"

He glanced over. "I have a first-aid kit. Warm cloths will help ease the tension in the muscle." Hoping to impart his intentions—that his son needed to shoulder a bit of independence—he held her gaze for an extra beat before continuing, "Dan, this is serious. Please hurry." He turned the boy toward the house. "Go."

The child's bottom lip quivered. "Daddy—"

"There's nothing to be afraid about. Quick, now."

Lee stepped forward. "I'll go with you, Danny."

"That isn't necessary." Oh, Rogan understood what was going on with his son. He understood the unease, the need to cling to the familiar. Hadn't *he* gone through an identical edginess five days ago boarding that seaplane?

"Actually, it is necessary," Lee said around a smile that said *I know this, I've seen it in you.* "We'll be right back."

Taking Danny's hand, she walked toward the farm-house

Frustrated, Rogan debated whether to order her back, but Addie Dalton was in pain and he had never avoided those in need. Assisting the underdog, the helpless, timid, wounded and vulnerable, they were the reasons he'd gone into law.

"Do as Ms. Tait says," he called as they walked away, through strips of fog.

Lee lifted her hand in response and an unfamiliar emotion crashed into his chest. Not wanting to scrutinize its cause, he turned and broke into a run toward the fence, wondering with every step if he was racing to Addie…or running from Lee.

Lee understood exactly what was going on with Rogan's son. It was easy to read the apprehension in the child's voice, the tension in his bony shoulders. She had witnessed the same sort of trepidation in his father climbing aboard her plane—that facing-the-unknown apprehension.

Whether Danny cloned Rogan's demeanor wasn't the issue. Rogan had to change his own behavior before he should expect it of his son. Except she wasn't a psychologist—just a pilot. And Rogan Matteo wasn't her boyfriend, husband or significant other. He was an acquaintance, that was all.

Climbing the steps of the wide porch, she asked, "So, do you like your new home, Danny?"

"Sorta. I like Juniper and her baby Pepper best."

"The horses?"

"Uh-huh. They're in the pasture over there."

Yes, Lee had heard about the previous renters claiming they no longer wanted the animals, leaving them behind when they moved to Spokane. Eve Riley, owner of the property and living in Oregon for the past twelve years, had agreed to keep the horses, then sold them as part of the farm.

"I love horses." Lee trailed Danny inside.

The three words were a hit.

Chattering about his favorite animals, the boy searched out the washcloths as she headed for the kitchen, which local contractor Zeb Jantz had reconstructed into a spacious country affair with Quaker cupboards, green wainscoting and yellow-patterned tiles. The floor space beside a tall, wide window looking out across the pasture held an ancient oak table and four ladder-backed chairs. Rogan clearly enjoyed furnishings of past eras.

But what caught her eye was the corner sink where a greenhouse window drew in an abundance of natural light. Her heart tugged at the sight of a lone dandelion in a glass of water on the wide sill. *Danny,* she thought and imagined his small fingers plucking the weedy flower to cheer up his father in their new house.

Here in this kitchen, a woman could dream and for a moment, just a moment, she let the dream slip into shape. She saw herself cooking at the modern replica of a 1930s-style stove. She pictured Rogan and Danny eating at the scarred table.

Making memories. With her.

"Is this enough?" Danny hurried into the room, snapping the dream shut.

He held at least ten washcloths.

"Perfect." Hiding a smile, she stacked them on the counter beside the sink, plugged the drain and ran the water until steam drifted off its surface.

"Do you know the sick lady?" A lock of blond hair fell into Danny's brown eyes as he studied the rising water.

"I do. She's my youngest sister."

"I used to have a sister older'n me. She died."

"Yes, honey." Lee glanced down at his earnest face. "Your daddy told me."

"Sophie was kinda bossy sometimes. Do you boss your sister?"

He said it with such seriousness that she chuckled. "Sometimes. Today I made her sit and rest until her husband comes to drive her home."

Danny dropped a washcloth into the water. His shoulder brushed her arm. "How come he wasn't with her?"

"Because walking is something my sisters and I do by ourselves."

"Don't you get lonely by yourself?"

"No, sometimes being by myself gives me a chance to do the things I like and enjoy."

"My mom liked shopping. She was always shopping with Sophie. They bought nice clothes and stuff."

And what did your mom buy you, little guy? Lee couldn't imagine the woman coming home empty-handed to this small replica of Rogan. Except for the light hair, the dark eyes, Danny Matteo favored his father in every way: high-boned cheeks, black lashes, straight mouth, the curve outlining his nose. And young as he was, his feet were already long and sturdy, his hands big.

He'd grow into his father's height and size. Soon, teenage girls would giggle behind their hands, and later women would send him come-hither looks.

She had never been one of those girls, one of those women.

She'd been the girl with freckled cheeks and arms; the one playing center in the basketball court because of her ability to jump as aggressively for the ball as the center on the boys' team.

She hadn't dated until her final year, hadn't had sex until her twenty-third birthday. She hadn't wanted to follow her mother's footsteps. Three men, three daughters.

And I will *be telling* my *baby about* her *daddy.*

Secreting away a father's name as Charmaine had with Kat was wrong, completely wrong.

Lee visualized Danny's mother—small-boned, gentle disposition, the perfect mother. Of course, she would've had flaws. Maybe one had been the shopping sprees Danny mentioned. But Mrs. Matteo would've been beautiful; a loving wife. Lee knew it, felt it as if the woman stood in this kitchen gazing over her shoulder.

Rogan had loved his wife. He missed her, *mourned* her.

"There's Daddy!" The boy rushed from the sink where he'd been swirling the washcloths with a spoon in the heated water.

Lee glanced through the garden window. Rogan strode across the pasture, Addie in his arms, Kat walking quickly at his side.

Behind her, the door banged closed. The next instant, she watched Danny dash across the yard toward the barn gate, and open the little wooden structure for his father.

Lee rushed out of the house. Had Addie fainted? Injured herself further? "What happened?" she called.

"Rogan's playing hero." Addie rolled her eyes, yet clung to his neck as he approached the porch steps.

"She couldn't walk all the way here," he clarified. "As it is, it's going to be a while before the muscle feels loose and normal again." He took the steps, shouldered through the door and walked straight into his kitchen where he helped Addie sit on one of the chairs at the old wooden table.

Crouching in front of their sister, Kat pushed up the hem of Addie's yoga pants and began massaging her calf muscle. "Stretch it as much as you can," she coaxed while Lee wrung out two heated washcloths. She handed them to Kat to press against the taut muscle.

"Can you point your toe upward?" Rogan asked. "That'll soften the knot and alleviate the pain to a degree."

"We did that on the trail," Lee informed him.

"Good." With Addie sitting and Lee and Kat hovering, he seemed at a loss as to what to do with three women in his house. "I'll wait outside for Skip. C'mon, Dan."

"He's a nice guy," Addie whispered when the door

closed behind the Matteo pair. "You won't go wrong with him, Lee. If you're interested."

"I'm not," she retorted, rinsing out another cloth.

Kat snorted. "Ask if her fingers are tingling."

"Your fingers tingle?"

"Whenever he's around," Kat said.

"Hush." Lee glanced at the door. "He'll hear you."

Addie frowned. "You *are* attracted to him."

"Not at all."

Kat let out a chuckle. "You are so in denial."

A vehicle rumbled outside. "Skip's here," Lee said. *Thank God.*

Addie leaned back in the chair. "I wish this hadn't happened. He's been after me to quit these walks for two months."

"Because he's crazy about you," Lee said.

"The feeling's mutual. But ever since I got pregnant, he's been worse than a protective pit bull."

"I'll talk to him." Relieved to end the conversation, Lee went out onto the porch. "She's fine," she said as the two tall men standing next to Skip's car turned in unison toward her.

Addie's husband took the porch steps in two bounds. "Damn it, why doesn't she use our home treadmill so I'm right there if something happens? She shouldn't be trail-hiking at this stage."

Lee caught his arm. "Don't make a big deal about it, Skip. She's feeling guilty enough as it is."

The misery in his eyes eased. "I'm worried sick about her."

"I know, but your reaction won't help. Trust me, she's healthy as a horse—well, except for the muscle cramp. Allow her some options about her exercise routine. And be willing to listen."

"Got it." He gave her a quick hug; paused to nod to Rogan. "I owe you, man." Then he vanished inside.

Rogan climbed the stairs, stopped on the step below Lee. "You're a great sister."

"Sometimes." Her gaze went to the soft dirt around the base of the old oak. On his knees, Danny designed tiny roads with a Tonka bulldozer.

"You worry about your family," Rogan remarked.

"Always."

"And that's what makes you different." His eyes were the mists loitering in the hollows of the pasture.

"You'd do the same for your son."

"Yes," he admitted. "But there are those who…" He shook his head. "It no longer matters."

Those who don't? she wondered. His wife, perhaps? *You're reading too much into his sad eyes, Lee.*

Her heart quickening, she took a step toward the door, away from him. "I need to help my sisters."

Five minutes later, Skip assisted Addie into their car. Standing beside Rogan and Danny, Lee watched her sisters and brother-in-law drive off. Skip would drop Kat at her B and B.

Because the distance was barely a mile, Lee opted to walk the trail back to her apartment.

"Danny and I'll walk with you," Rogan said. The sun broke through tendrils of fog to gloss his black hair with streaks of blue.

"Thank you," Lee said, "but I'll be fine. I enjoy walking."

"So do we." Eyes glinting with humor, he turned to

his son. "Grab your bike, buddy. We're walking Ms. Tait back to her place."

The boy ran for his mountain bike parked at the side of the house. "We're walking in the woods, Dad?" Danny asked, hopping onto the seat and pedaling hard into the yard.

"Yes, but be careful crossing the pasture," Rogan called as he and Lee watched the child race toward the barn. "There are rocks and holes and…" His voice trailed off. "Bumps."

Lee couldn't help chuckle. "The rougher the better, didn't you know, Dad? It's what boys thrive on." Certainly those she'd grown up with. Oliver had been one of those boys.

"Danny's not most boys." Rogan started toward the gate.

"From what I've seen he's very much your typical boy."

"He had a hard time dealing with his mother's and sister's deaths."

"Him? Or you?" The words were out before she realized she'd spoken aloud. "I'm sorry, Rogan. I don't know why I said that."

Once, twice, his arm brushed hers as they walked. He said, "Truth is, these past years have been damned hard. From one day to the next I don't know how I'm supposed to act. Should I be a dad today? A mom tomorrow? Obviously I can't *be* his mother—or his sister, for that matter. I can only be me." He exhaled hard. "Too often I feel inadequate."

They came to the gate and he held it open for Danny to pedal through. "Don't go near the horses," Rogan warned. "The bike might scare them."

"Okay." Keeping vigil on the mare and her foal, Danny rode cautiously forward.

Lee longed to tell Rogan to give the boy some slack. The horses were several acres away, in a far corner; the mare grazed unconcerned, the foal lay dozing nearby in the grass. Neither paid attention to the boy on his bike.

Watching Danny's over-sensitized worry about the animals—a worry established, she believed, by a father who blamed himself for the tragedy in his family—Lee had to force herself to remember the boy was not her child.

Her child was…*here.*

Fisting her fingers over her still-flat belly, she wondered what Rogan would think if she told him. Did she care?

Oddly, yes. She cared a great deal.

They walked to the pasture gate on the far side of the property. Back on the wooded trail she and her sisters had traveled, she said, "I think it's normal to feel inadequate when you're trying to raise a child alone."

Heck, her baby was barely the size of her pinky finger and apprehension bloomed. Apprehension she might not be mother enough. That she might fail in some way because no one would be there to catch her if she fell, the way Skip had been here for Addie minutes before.

Of course, he hadn't always been. Lee knew Addie had been overwhelmed and fiercely alone during her first pregnancy. But she'd survived, gotten through it and look where she was today.

Rogan broke through Lee's contemplation. "It's more than feeling inadequate," he said. "It's the fear something will happen and he'll be left alone."

His hand brushed the sleeve of her sweatshirt, so she moved until an imperceptible gap lay between them. His head turned, and his gray eyes were dark as the woods they walked. "I don't know what it is, but when I'm with you, I seem to breathe easier."

She wanted to cajole, "Don't be silly." But she said nothing, her tongue unable to form a sound.

They walked around the bend. Up ahead, a clifflike path hidden by ferns, vines and undergrowth slanted down two hundred feet to the beach. Lee and her sisters had often branched off the main trail to wander the rocky shore below, seeking colored stones or shells or driftwood, or to simply enjoy the battering waves, the distant sights of ferries and boats, the gulls wheeling and dipping.

Danny skidded the bike to a stop and before Lee could call out, the boy zipped into the brush and vanished.

"Daniel!" Rogan ran forward, his long legs chewing the distance in three seconds.

His fear spurred Lee into a sprint.

Down the side path she went, digging her heels into the damp earth as she followed the steep, junglelike path behind Rogan. Dew clung to overhanging branches and wet her face.

Together they shot from the thick bank of undergrowth, almost tripping over Danny, who stood on a sliver of sand edging the stony shoreline. The sea lapped at the beach a mere twenty feet away.

"Daniel." Rogan voice was low, stern.

The child turned. "Look, Dad. Look at those cool birds." He pointed left to where a pair of Pacific loons stood on a cluster of large rocks. Under a sluggish sun smoldering away the mist, the birds ignored the human invasion and continued preening themselves in the morning warmth.

Disregarding the waterfowl, Rogan strode forward. "Son, why did you go off the trail?"

"'Cause," he sing-songed. "I wanted to be brave like you said."

"Aw, buddy. You're the bravest boy I know. But what if this path had dropped straight into the ocean like they sometimes do?"

The boy hung his head. "I'd be in the water."

Rogan crouched down and pushed blond strands off the boy's forehead. "Yeah. You would be."

"But I can swim. And so can you," Danny added eagerly.

"We can," Rogan agreed. "But if there was a tide, it could take you way, way out to sea before I'd get to you. Tides are much stronger than we are."

"Are they dangerous?"

"If you're not familiar with them."

Danny's brown eyes were full of guilt.

Unable to stop herself, Lee curled her fingers over Rogan's shoulder. He turned his gaze up to hers. "I think," he said gently to his son. "We've learned enough here. Let's go back up to the trail."

Hauling the bike to his shoulder, he took Lee's hand and together they climbed the long path through the leafy brushwood. When they were on the upper trail again, he set the bike down and ruffled his son's hair. "Next time, we'll go together, maybe look for some seashells, okay, pal?

"Yeah!" Danny's face brightened. "Can I pedal ahead now?"

"Sure, but stay in sight, all right?" When the boy rode out of earshot, he studied Lee's hand in his. "Guess I get a little carried away at parenting."

"No," she said. "Danny needed to know the difference."

"I've gotten a little paranoid these last few years."

"I understand." And she did. Already she'd become more cautious with the baby under her heart. Watching Danny pedal down the trail, she said, "You have a sweet son. Why not take him shell-seeking right now? He'll love it."

"Will you come with us?"

"I can't." He needed time with his son, time to collect seashells. Gently, reluctantly, she extracted her hand from his. "Thanks for the invite, though, and for walking me this far."

"Lee…"

Walking backward, she gave him a little wave, then turned and jogged slowly up the path. When she reached his child, she said, "You were a great help in the kitchen, Danny."

"Where you goin'?" he asked.

"Got some work to do. Go see your dad, I think you guys are going to look for shells."

"We are? Yay!"

Lee grinned and pushed herself into an easy stride, and tried not to think of Rogan's arms holding her sister, or the way his voice soothed his son's fears—or how his hand had engulfed hers and kept her steady while they climbed up a steep, rocky cliff path.

Chapter Six

"How's the new house?" Johnny asked that afternoon. "Everything all sorted out? Is Danny happy?"

Cell phone to his ear, Rogan walked onto the porch of the farmhouse and sat in one of the two handcrafted rockers he'd bought at The Old Wood Store. Below the porch railing, he could hear Danny's *brrrrom-brrrrom* as he shoved toy trucks and bulldozers through the dirt around the budding hydrangea plants in the flowerbed.

"Everything's going as planned," Rogan told his brother. "Most of the important boxes are unpacked. We're tackling Dan's room first, though."

"Good to hear. I still think it's a crazy decision, but then who am I to say what's right or wrong."

"Exactly. You don't have a say."

"Touchy today?"

"We've been through this before." Much as he wanted to talk to Johnny, Rogan would rather his brother leave the home and hearth questions out of the conversation. "Anything new?"

"Matter of fact there is. I might have a case for you."

Rogan perked up. "Yeah?"

"Desert Storm pilot lives on your island. Claims his disability pension has been cut back for no reason, except to save the government money."

"Tell him to give me a call and that it'll be *pro bono*." Because their father had lost an arm and an eye in Vietnam, Rogan never charged a penny to veterans.

"Thanks, Ro. His name's Peyton Sawyer."

"Got it." He leaned forward, elbows to knees. "Any news on my issue?"

"Actually, yeah. Got a call this morning about someone who used to work for Abner Air."

"Who?"

"Let me explore it a little further, okay? I don't want you to go off half-cocked and hunt this person down."

Rogan stared at the leafing trees sheltering the road into his farmhouse. Johnny was right. He *would* hunt down the person—and jeopardize the investigation by saying the wrong thing, or worse.

Rubbing his eyes, he released a breath of air. "I wish this were over."

"It will be."

"No," Rogan murmured so Danny couldn't hear. "It'll never be over. Their deaths will always be here." He thumped his chest as if Johnny could see the gesture. "Right here."

"That's because you blame yourself. You need to let go, man. Better yet, find yourself a woman, get some action."

Rogan snorted. "Anyone ever tell you you're a crass son of a bitch?"

Johnny chuckled. "You, mostly."

They spoke a few minutes more about Rogan's plans for the property before setting a weekend in May when Johnny would be available to visit Firewood Island and see the new house.

After shutting the cell phone, Rogan remained on the porch, listening to Danny mutter his civil engineering plans for the flowerbed. A sense of peace flowed through him. Regardless of what his brother presumed, he *had* made the right choice moving Danny onto these few acres. The boy would heal here.

And maybe, just maybe, Rogan would, too.

Find yourself a woman, get some action.

Much as he hated to admit it, Johnny had a point. A woman could obliterate the past, even for a couple hours.

But not any woman, Rogan thought, as a vision of red hair and green eyes bloomed into his brain. *She* could make him forget.

Lee.

The way she'd looked this morning in his pasture with the mist floating around her ankles…

Suddenly antsy, he rose and stepped to the railing. "Danny, don't—" The words died as an image of her standing on the wooded trail, eyes full of sympathy for him and Danny flashed across his mind. Pity wasn't what he wanted from her. No, what he wanted was to…*get some action.* Scraping a hand through hair, Rogan groaned. *Hell.*

"Don't what, Dad?" Danny gazed up, a Mariners ballcap shading his dark eyes.

"Don't get too close to the roses. They have thorns. You got some fine roads and highways there, bud. Don't change them until we take a picture."

Danny's grin stretched ear-to-ear. "Okay!"

A thumbs up, Rogan chuckled. For the first time today, he felt good. Damn good. "See you in a bit."

Returning to the kitchen where he'd been organizing the dishes in the cupboards before Johnny's call, he began whistling an old John Denver tune, *Take Me Home, Country Roads*—and wondered if Lee would ever take him home.

While Lee puttered around her plane and then her apartment, she thought of the Matteos. How did their house look after a day of arranging and decorating? Had they hung pictures on the bare walls, laid rugs on the aged hardwood?

She liked Rogan's taste in furniture. Over the years, she had become an amateur antique buff when it came to teapots. She loved their elegance, the intricate styles and hand-painted decorative designs. Five years ago, she purchased a turn-of-the-century Shaker corner cupboard to exhibit the delicate chinaware.

To their friends, her ex had called the display her "woman's thing"—as if he were patting Lee on the head. He'd considered the remark humorous. She had not. The teapots signified what she'd missed: a past with her father.

Washing her dinner plate in the sink, she looked back at the garage sale cupboard that she'd worked two months to restore. On the top shelf sat a lone teapot, the one her dad had given her mother on their wedding day.

Drying her hands on the towel, Lee walked to the cabinet. Circa 1880, the teapot was beautifully crafted with an exquisite garden scene on each side.

Once, long ago, she had asked her mother the reason behind Steven Tait's gift. Charmaine had shrugged and said, "Maybe he figured I liked tea."

But Lee had seen the pain in her mother's eyes. There was more than indifference behind the story. After all, Steven Tait had left when Lee was a toddler. Walked out the door one sunny day, never to return.

Studying the china piece, she wondered again how a man could demonstrate the sappiness—or sentimentality—to buy a teapot, and yet leave his wife and child. For the thousandth time, she pushed aside the strangeness of the circumstance. According to Charmaine, marriage to Steven Tait had been a series of shouting matches. Lee recalled none, but then she'd been just three years old.

Sighing, she returned to the kitchen, hung the towel on the stove handle and put away the dinner dishes.

On her way to the couch to watch a sitcom, her gaze lingered on the counter and the toy digger she'd purchased today for Danny. Danny, who loved building roads in the dirt. Beside the miniature machine stood the triple-herb tray she'd bought an hour later with Rogan's sunny kitchen window in mind. Oh, yes, she could see the plants—basil, rosemary and peppermint—happily enjoying streams of sunshine lighting the windows. Tomorrow she'd offer the gifts as a welcome to their new home, but more importantly as a token of gratitude for helping Addie.

Picking up the phone, Lee curled into a corner of the sofa and dialed her sister's number.

"Hey," she said when Addie answered. "How's the leg?"

"Great. The cramping is gone. The massaging and hot cloths really helped."

"The cloths were Rogan's idea."

"Oh, don't remind me. I was so embarrassed when he carried me to the house. Me weighing ten tons and all."

Lee could hear Skip in the background. "Only nine tons, sweetheart."

"Go away," Addie said to her husband, but Lee heard the smacking kiss, the little moan. "I'm going into the study," Addie told her. "Where I can have some peace."

Lee chuckled.

"Now, where were we?" Addie said with a small grunt and Lee pictured her settling in the big lounger in the Daltons' study. "Oh, yeah. Rogan lugging me across that pasture like a poor pack mule."

Lee laughed. "Oh, I don't think you bothered him in the least. He's a strong man."

"Huh. So you're admitting I'm a whale?"

"No, honey. I'm saying you're a pregnant woman."

"I am," Addie said happily. "But…I have to know…"

"What?"

"Rogan," Addie whispered. "Does he have a nice butt?"

Lee sputtered. "Addie!"

"Well, I never got to see. He was always facing me or carrying me."

"Better than Skip's," Lee remarked, lips tweaking.

"Okay, hold it right there. No one has a better butt than Skip."

"Depends on who's looking."

"I *knew* it," Addie said smugly. "You more than like the man. So are you going to ask him out?"

Lee laughed. "Argh. You were setting me up just now."

"Yup." A grin drifted through the line. "By the way, Skip wants to take Rogan and his son to a Mariners game once the season starts. Sort of a thank you for what he did for me today."

"An offer I'm sure he won't turn down."

"So, *will* you ask him out?"

Lee shook her head. "He's a nice guy, but that's where it ends. I have no interest in him—now or later." *Liar, then why were you thinking about him all day?*

"Lee," Addie said. "If there's a connection, why not go for it?"

"Have you forgotten I'm pregnant?" Never mind her history with Abner Air, a company, she realized now, that had neglected to do a background check on a certain pilot. A company that had put Rogan through hell.

"What does having a pleasant dinner or going to a movie have to do with being pregnant?" her sister asked.

"Nothing. But I'm not you, Addie. I can't pretend everything's hunky-dory." Lee sighed. "Damn it. I'm sorry. Your situation fourteen years ago was entirely different."

"Yes," her sister conceded. "It was. Skip and I were teenagers manipulated by our parents. You, on the other hand, are an independent, successful woman." Her voice softened. "Don't be so scared, Lee. Until you start showing, go have some fun. Heck, by then he'll be so crazy about you, he won't be able to walk away."

"I'm not going to trick him, Addie."

"Of course, you aren't. Tell him up front and if it makes a difference to him, then he wasn't the one. But if it doesn't…"

"I could do worse, that it?"

"Possibly. Though I think it's unlikely. However, you'll never know unless you take the step."

When she crawled under the covers that night, Lee mulled over Addie's advice. *Take the step.* Hadn't she done that with Stuart? With Oliver? And where had it got her?

Pregnant and beside herself with worry she would lose this baby—along with her business.

Her sisters were wrong. Adding a man to the mix was just plain dumb. Especially a man linked to her in a horrible twist of fate.

Still, when the clock on her nightstand indicated the midnight hour, the anticipation of giving her gifts to Rogan and his son had yet to subside.

Shortly after lunch the following day, she parked in front of his farmhouse. Strange, but already she thought of the property as "Rogan's place," and no longer "the old Riley farm."

The sun blazed warm and bright over the pasture's southerly woods as Lee stepped from her Jeep.

Country quiet settled into her bones. Somewhere a bird warbled a melody while a light breeze shifted the hair she'd left loose on her shoulders. A spice of nature—damp earth, ripe buds, new grass—pulled her senses. *I could live here,* she thought.

The notion startled her. She'd never been the "country" type. Not in music or entertainment and certainly not in choosing a place to reside. Her idea of home was a house or apartment amidst civilization, with a blend of trendy and old décor, and easy access to whatever shops and restaurants she required.

So why was she feeling this…this sense of home-coming on a piece of land she had known about since age six when she and Eve Riley entered first grade?

Lee sighed. The pregnancy was playing silly games with her hormones and common sense.

Except hadn't she told Rogan his house was lovely? That she admired his traditional furnishings, the old-fashioned herb window?

Standing beside the Jeep, she glanced at the toy digger, the tray of herb plants waiting on the passenger seat. Her way of saying *I understand your home.*

"Lee!"

She turned at the sound of his call.

He stood with Danny in the doorway of the weathered little barn. Lifting a hand in greeting, she started across the yard, noting the splatters and smears of paint on their ratty jeans and sweatshirts as she approached. Mariner ballcaps protected their hair and sheltered their eyes, although a couple of white fingerprints dotted Danny's visor.

Suddenly, she felt overdressed in her pencil-style black skirt, calf-high black stiletto boots and belted woolen jacket the color of curry. What was she thinking, wearing going-to-dinner clothes to a farm? Before she could stop herself, a nervous laugh pocked the air. "I was in the neighborhood…"

Striding forward, Rogan broke into a pleased grin. "I was going to call you. I need to catch another flight with you tomorrow."

"To Renton?"

"Yep." His eyes swallowed her whole.

Flustered, she said, "I brought you something. For Danny, too."

"Did you now?" His gaze held hers.

"A sort of welcome token for your new home, and for helping Addie."

"Can't wait to see it." He stopped within arm's reach. The grin remained. "We were just talking about you. Weren't we, Dan?"

"You were?" Oh, but his eyes were beautiful. The deep gray of evening, moments before the moon rose.

"Uh-huh." Danny nodded. "Dad thinks your hair smells nice. He says it reminds him of strawberry jam."

Rogan pulled playfully at the visor of his son's cap. "I said no such thing."

"Did so, Dad. And you said it looks like a bunch of copper wire, too."

Lee bit the inside of her cheek to thwart a bubble of laughter. "Copper wire, huh? Sounds like a great style for a lady."

"Danny means the *color* is like copper wire. I mean, I said its color is…" He shook his head, laughed. "Okay, can I dig this hole any deeper?"

"What hole, Dad?"

"Never mind, son."

Lee gazed at the man who swam through her dreams. He liked her hair. Well, in her case he liked wire—and jam. No one had bothered to compare her to anything before. She didn't know whether to hug him or walk away.

"Know what?" he said. "Let's start over. Hello, Lee."

Her lips hitched. "Hey, guys." She nodded to the paint-weary barn. "Sprucing things up?"

"We are," Rogan said. "Come see."

They walked into the quaint, hip-roofed building with its lingering scent of old hay and manure. The interior contained a couple of horse stalls and—from the appearance of the wooden waist-high cubbies attached to a wall—a pen where chickens once laid eggs. From the narrow side windows, sunshine laced the center aisle and illuminated a spattering of lazy dust motes.

Rogan went through the barn to the open rear doors. "We're testing our skills on the exterior wall. That way," he winked down at his son, "nobody will see our first errors."

"Good plan." Outside, Lee noted the scaffolding, the pails of white and barn-red paint; the two brushes—one large, one small.

"Danny's job is the sign." Rogan pointed to a long, thin plank jacked between two sawhorses. One side had already been painted white. Or as white as a seven-year-old could make.

Lee touched the boy's shoulder. "A very hard job, too."

Something flickered in Rogan's eyes. Had she offended him? Did he think she wanted the boy playing instead of working?

He said, "We're hanging the sign above the front doors of the barn so anyone coming into the yard can see it. The lettering will be red to match the exterior."

So. He was putting his stamp on the place by giving it a name. "And what's it going to be called?"

"We're not sure yet. Dan wants to make a list." Rogan watched the boy wander to the fence. In the middle of the pasture, the mare stood dozing in the sun while her foal nursed. "He thought of calling it Juniper and Pepper's Farm, but that was too long for the plank, so we abbreviated it to… Ah, hell." He rubbed the back of his neck. "I have no idea why I'm rambling on about a bunch of boring junk."

Lee smiled. "It's all interesting."

Rogan slanted her a look. "You're a classy lady, know that? Any other woman would've been yawning by now."

His wife, perhaps? Not a topic to pursue. She said, "I never grew up on a farm, but a childhood friend used to live here, so seeing her old place go through a resurrection of sorts has special meaning."

For a long moment he said nothing, just looked at her. "What?"

"I'm adding one-of-a-kind to classy."

"Don't make me into something I'm not, Rogan."

"Is that what I'm doing?"

"Yes. There's more underneath this jacket than a few words." She recognized her mistake the instant she closed her mouth.

"I couldn't agree more." His gaze moved over her body before returning to her face. "I've been a widower for three years. I have a kid, so I don't get out much—

which, I'm sure, shows through my sparkling wit. But even if I did go out with women, I'd still think you were one-of-a-kind."

She scoffed softly. "Yes, most men see female pilots that way. A woman in a man's world, that sort of thing."

"It has nothing to do with you flying planes, Lee."

"Well," she said, unconvinced. "Shall we quit this discussion and see what I brought you both?"

He kept his eyes on hers for a handful of beats. Then, he turned his head. "Danny. Get down from the fence. You're bothering the horses."

During their conversation, Lee saw that the mare had wandered in from the pasture. Tail switching flies, she stood a few feet from the fence. Hiding under its mother's chin, the foal gazed curiously at Danny.

"I'm not doing anything," the boy said, clinging to the top of the fence. "Please, Daddy. I want to pet them."

Rogan strode to his son. "They're not familiar with us yet. I want you down off that fence."

Lee frowned. "Have you ever ridden a horse, Danny?"

The boy's eyes lit. "Uh-uh. Daddy, can I ride Juniper?"

"No. Now come down off the fence."

"Aw…" Reluctantly, Danny descended. "How come I can't ride Juniper?"

"I took lessons when I was a kid," Lee pointed out, her heart wavering at the dejection in the child's eyes.

Rogan shot her a look that said *please don't encourage him.*

She wanted to tell him not to impose his fears onto his son. She wanted to tell him to let the child breathe, not to smother him with his worries.

None of your business, Lee.

"Can you show me how to ride, Ms. Tait?" the boy asked.

"Not right now, son," Rogan interjected. Then his eyes softened. "She has something to show us."

"You do?" Danny asked eagerly, all thought of horses and riding gone. "What is it?"

"Why don't you come and see. It's in the Jeep."

Danny ran through the barn and out the front doors.

"I'm sorry," Rogan murmured beside her as they walked through the barn. "About the riding stuff."

"You know your son best."

"But you don't agree."

The squared toes of his work boots were tough and inflexible. "Whether I agree isn't important," she said. "If people concurred every time, we'd still be in the Paleozoic period."

"Interesting analogy. You think I'm that obstinate?"

Instead of answering, she opened the truck's passenger door, and took out the digger for the boy. "I didn't see one of these when you were building by the oak tree the other day."

Danny's eyes lit. "A digger! Dad, she got me a digger!"

Rogan's features relaxed. "What do you say?"

"Thank you, Miss Tait! Can I go play, Dad?"

"You bet."

The child's delight pleased Lee. Reaching back into the Jeep, she drew out the container of herbs. "For your greenhouse window," she said, handing him the specialized three-tiered pot.

He blinked. "My greenhouse window? Oh, you mean that window extension over the sink? I asked Zeb to remodel the kitchen into a room with light." An edge of his mouth turned up. "Seems I have a lot to learn about farming, including growing a garden."

"I could help," Lee said. What was she doing? She didn't know the first inkling about farming, never mind planting garden seeds. Her skills in that department sat in pots similar to the one he held, nurtured by a horticulturalist.

"Help I can always use," Rogan replied. "Sure you want to work with a hard-headed, obstinate guy?" he teased.

He was referring to her prior comment about his behavior around Danny.

"Not hard-headed," she said around a little laugh. "Just a little over-anxious. Normal, after what you've gone through."

Around her, the temperature dropped ten degrees. "What I've gone through," he said softly, "is pure unadulterated hell." His eyes pierced. "Do you know what hell is, Lee?"

"Maybe not the kind you mean. But I have lost my footing through other ways." Hoping for a family that never evolved and a husband who chose affairs as a solution. Burying a best friend turned lover.

"It's not an easy road," she went on, "but you travel it because it's the only route you have."

"What I want is for my boy not to miss his mother and sister. I want something good for him."

Lee observed the child digging in the dirt. "It'll happen. You've made an excellent choice settling him here, Rogan. This place will heal him." *And you,* she thought. *Most of all you.*

"My brother thinks I made a mistake."

"Do you?"

"No."

"Well then. As they say in your world…case closed." She opened the driver's door of the SUV, nodded to the container in his hands. "Have fun spicing."

"Why not stay for lunch, share the taste testing?"

"Maybe another time." She climbed behind the wheel. "You know how it goes. Things to do, people to see, places to go."

He stepped into the door she had yet to pull shut. "I've scared you off with my reaction about my past."

She laughed lightly. "That's where you're wrong, Rogan." *Because I'm a sucker for wounded men I've scared myself off.* "The only thing that scares me is the thought of planting your garden. See you tomorrow." When she'd fly him across the Sound for his work.

With a nod, he moved out of the way and she shut the door.

Yes, she thought, watching him grow smaller in the rearview mirror. For her, the case of the Matteos was definitely closed. She glanced down at her stomach. "You," she said to the baby, "are all that matters."

Chapter Seven

The following week, Rogan made two more business trips to the mainland in Lee's plane. While there wasn't much discussion on board—not while a lump continued to plug his throat—he admitted he *was* getting better about climbing into the cockpit. She made the flights easier with her relaxed demeanor, her knowledge of planes, with the way her freckled hands worked the controls, and the fact her bright curly hair drove him crazy.

After cutting the engine at Burnt Bend's wharf on Thursday afternoon, she climbed from the seaplane and handed him his briefcase. "See you around."

A stone hit his gut. He didn't look forward to the four-day gap between now and next Monday. He wanted to see her every day. He wanted to hear her voice and watch her eyes change with the topic of conversation.

He wanted to hold her hand.

To kiss her.

There were a hundred things he wanted with Lee Tait. And none, he knew, would come to fruition because he was a single father whose first priority was his son—and last Sunday Rogan had acted like an ass.

So he stood on the dock, debating, while she opened the cargo hatch. Fitz from the coffee shop pulled his truck into the tiny gravel parking lot a rock's toss away. In another minute, the man would approach with a flatbed trolley to haul away Lee's load of expedited mail and freight boxes.

"Forget something?" she asked, reaching in to tug the first package forward.

Definitely not. "No, but I wish you'd let me help."

"Not necessary." She climbed into the hold.

"I know. Fitz's job." Still, Rogan wanted to do something for her. Twice this week, while he sat beside her in the cockpit, that something had been on his mind. He hadn't liked the way he'd snapped at her last Sunday. *Do you know what hell is?* he'd asked as if she were stupid. As if she didn't understand the weight on his shoulders.

Lee Tait was not stupid. She saw right through him, and maybe that was why he sat on a teeter-totter of emotion today.

Much as he'd loved Darby, Lee saw him in ways his late wife had not. She sensed his moods, his intentions, his hurt. He had no idea how; they were just getting to know each other, but there it was. She understood what made him tick. And that scared the hell out of him— even though he couldn't stop thinking about her halfway into every night.

"Have a nice weekend," he said at last.

"You, too." She offered a quick smile he tucked into his heart. Turning, he walked down the boardwalk, nodded as he passed Fitz dragging the trolley to the anchored plane.

He had taken maybe thirty steps when he heard Lee call his name. Swinging around, Rogan watched her advance, a woman of adventure and success, who knew what she wanted in life. A woman in a dark flight jacket with its wing insignia above her left breast, moving with the grace of a ballerina.

She stopped close enough for him to catch the scent of strawberries in her hair. Her eyes were the greenest he'd seen; the ring around the irises black as night.

"Would you and Danny like a home-cooked meal Friday evening?" she asked.

Looking into her upturned face, he felt the boardwalk tilt ever so slightly. God, he had it bad for her.

Unbinding his tongue, he said, "Danny would like that. He's been complaining about my cooking."

"And what about you?" Her brows rose in mirth.

"I eat whatever's on the table."

"Good. Then I'll see you at six." She turned to go. "By the way, we're having chicken *cacciatore*."

"Looking forward to it. And, Lee? Thanks."

Her smile steamed his blood. "This isn't only for you, Rogan."

"No?"

He drank in the sound of her laughter. "I'll leave it at that. See you in a couple days, Mr. Lawyer."

He watched her walk back to her plane before he continued toward the small-town office he'd opened.

Twenty-four hours and he'd see her again. Twenty-four hours…for him to turn five words, *this isn't only for you,* inside out and upside down in search of her meaning. One thing was certain. She had wrapped the words in the most sultry voice he'd ever heard.

At noon on Friday, after she returned from a flight to Bremerton, Lee was ready for a power nap. Blaming it on the whims of the first trimester, she slowly climbed the stairs to her apartment. A sound above brought up her head. Rogan stood on the landing.

"Waiting for me?" she asked, shaking out her keys. She should be getting used to him working several steps away. This week she'd heard him moving furniture and opening and closing doors.

His appearance now set her body thrumming. Heavens, he was magnificent, standing there in a tan shirt with his maroon tie tugged loose. Already a day's beard growth darkened his cheeks and his hair was disheveled where his restless fingers had plowed. God help her, he looked sexier than any man she'd seen in ten years.

"I heard your plane so I wanted to say hi."

The landing forced them to stand close enough for her to feel crowded by his strong, sturdy body. A shiver rode her spine—not from fear—but from an awareness that spoke of sex and heat and secret words.

As if discerning that shiver, he shoved his hands into the pockets of his tailored black trousers. "Can I buy you lunch?" His nostrils flared slightly. Had he picked up her scent?

The key found home; she swung open her door as a

sudden wave of nausea exploded in her stomach. Praying she didn't look green, she said, "Thanks, but I'm not hungry." Oh, God, she needed the washroom *now*. "Excuse me."

Rushing into the apartment, she raced down the tiny hallway for the washroom. In the next second, she was dry heaving into the toilet.

"Lee?"

He had followed her because she'd forgotten to close the door.

Unable to speak, she held up a hand. *Please, go away.*

And then she had no time for thoughts, words or embarrassment. Her eyes watered, her stomach spun. Every ounce of energy focused on her poise over the bowl. Clutching the tank, she listened to her guttural heaves—and felt him pull her hair out of the way, his warm hand against her damp forehead.

"I'm here," was all he said.

Lee closed teary eyes. Yes, he was here, and for the moment she was grateful, so grateful. Later, she could think about the awkwardness of it all.

He waited until her stomach settled and her breathing no longer labored, before grabbing several tissues from the box on the toilet tank to wipe her eyes, her mouth. No doubt he'd done this before, with his wife.

"Thank you," Lee croaked.

"No problem." He took a washcloth, ran it under warm water and handed it to her. "I'll be in the living room."

She stared into the mirror. Was it the baby staking a claim on her body, or the burrito she'd had for lunch? Or was it just nerves? She glanced at the bottle of anti-nausea pills on the counter beside her toothbrush. Since last Saturday's trail walk with her sisters, Lee had been religious about following the doctor's orders.

No stress, Lily had said. *Easier said than done,* Lee thought. In seven months she would have a baby. And sooner than that, she needed to decide what to do about her plane and her business. And then there was the Abner Air situation involving Rogan....

Shutting her eyes, she inhaled slowly. *Relax, Lee. Everything will work out.* She had to believe that.

She reached for her toothbrush and, minutes later, returned to the living room. Rogan sat on her sofa the way a man would, slouched forward, knees spread, and reading one of the three flight magazines on her coffee table. At her approach, his head lifted. Their eyes locked.

Into the silence, she said, "I'm pregnant."

His features didn't change. He simply looked at her steadily, calmly. He didn't blurt *No way.* Or *I thought it might be a bug.* Or *Are you sure?* He said, "How far along?"

"A little over eight weeks." She expected him to jump to his feet, to say, *Well, nice knowing ya* and leave.

Instead, he closed the magazine without fuss, and rose. Then he walked over, stroked a knuckle along her cheek. "Why don't you sit for a minute and I'll make a cup of tea, get you some saltines."

He *had* done this before.

"Aren't you going to ask where the father is?"

"If he was important, Lee, you would've told me about him before now." He leaned in, laid his mouth on hers, chaste, tender and sweet.

Her eyes closed. His fingertips touched her brow. "Let's get you sitting down," he whispered.

Arm supporting her waist, he guided her to the sofa where she curled into a corner and pulled the blue-and-white afghan she'd knitted last winter across her feet. The sofa faced the boardwalk and cove. She had positioned the furniture so she could see the day first thing in the morning—and while she ate her meals or sipped her herbal teas.

Now, as she listened to Rogan work around her kitchen, her gaze centered on her plane and she tried not to think of the day she would need to give up flying. She tried, instead, to concentrate on telling Rogan where things were: the lavender tea, the cups and saucers, the crackers.

Within minutes, he brought a tray, sat across from her, and poured a cup. They sipped, contentedly without speaking before he said, "Tomorrow's dinner plans have changed."

Should she be surprised? He might be kind and generous with his help, but the attraction, that heat he'd exuded on the landing—and everywhere else—had vanished.

"I understand. Pregnant women aren't the greatest company, especially when they're upchucking."

He smiled. "*Au contraire.* Pregnant women are an adventure. What I meant is the dinner venue has changed. I'll cook for you at the farm instead of us coming here. I know—" He held up a hand. "You made the offer first, but circumstances being what they are, I'd like to do this. And anyway, Danny's anxious to show you the town he's made with the digger."

She pushed back the emotion in her throat. "I don't know what to say."

"Say yes, Lee." His gray eyes were sober. "This doesn't change things, you know."

She held her breath. "What things?"

"The way I feel about you."

"And how is that?"

He sighed, set down his cup, came around the table and sat beside her on the couch.

"Rogan—"

"Just listen for a minute, will you?" His gaze went to her hair, loose along her shoulders. He coiled a spiral around his finger, watched how the strand sprang when he released it. "I'm going to tell you something and I don't want you to feel sorry or pity me. It's just information, okay?"

"Okay." The air in her lungs thinned.

"I loved my wife very much. We had our differences, but she was a good woman, a good mother and when she and my daughter died…well, I went a little nuts. I didn't eat for days, didn't sleep, didn't feel like living. I blamed myself for their deaths. Still do. Darby was suffering from depression, and we… We were going through a difficult stage in our marriage. When she got on that plane with Sophie, she was flying across Olympic National Forest to Forks for her mother's birthday. I knew she planned to stay for a couple weeks. To sort things out, think things through. Danny had an ear infection at the time, so I booked a flight for him the following week."

"Rogan…"

"Darby hadn't wanted to fly in a small plane, but it was the only charter that flew to the Forks Quillayute Airport on a Tuesday."

A shudder crawled down Lee's back. No wonder he was so skittish flying with her.

"Anyway, that morning she didn't want to go. Said she didn't feel good about the trip. But she hadn't felt good about a lot of things, so I thought it was the depression talking."

He drew a deep breath. "I told her things would be fine, that the break would help us get some perspective. She'd be with family—sister, brother, parents—I was hoping like hell they could help us somehow." He paused, eyes resolute. "We'd been sleeping separately for almost a year."

Lee pressed a finger to his mouth. "Shhh. What's past is past."

He took her hand, kissed her fingertips. "It is, but it's also what makes us who we are today. I want you to know where I've come from, who I am."

"From what I've seen, you're a good father and a decent man. Nothing more matters."

He cupped her cheek; his eyes searched her face. "I'm so damned attracted to you. From that first evening I stood on the dock and watched you work on your plane, I knew."

She touched his lips with her thumb, slowly traced the sensuous outline. "Are you going to kiss me, Rogan?" she whispered.

He hesitated a mere second before he scooped her into his lap. "I'm going to kiss you for a long time, Lee." Dipping his head, he took her mouth in a kiss that electrified every cell, then deposited a hot, golden pool in her nether regions. A lingering kiss that evoked promises.

The shape of his mouth, how his tongue capered with hers, the way he tasted of the honey he'd stirred in his tea—all possessed her senses. And then, slowly, his fingers traveled into her hair and his lips nibbled, here and there, on a journey down her neck.

Oh, my, she thought. *Oh. My.*

He roamed her face, caressed her eyes, her brow and once more honed in on her mouth.

When, *when* had she been kissed like this?

Her sisters were right. She was starved. Sex-starved. Starved for Rogan. For his taste, touch, scent, for anything and everything that was him. Under her thighs, his urgency strengthened. And it sent her blood racing, her breath trembling.

Lifting his head, he smiled down at her. "I'm glad I moved to the island. I'm glad you're my pilot. I'm glad for a lot of things, but right now, Lee, I'm glad I'm here with you. Like this."

Again, a kiss. Soft, gentle, sweet and melting her heart.

He continued, "I'm going to take care of you."

The mellowness she felt ebbed suddenly. "I don't need taking care of."

"Of course, you don't, but I'd like to anyway."

She sat quietly for a moment, then squirmed out of his embrace and walked to the window. Arms hugging her middle, she turned to face him. He hadn't moved, except to lean forward and clasp his hands loosely between his knees.

Her mouth burned with the imprint of his. Her skin cried out for his touch. She wanted to rush back to him, back into his arms. Instead, she said, "I don't need an armored knight, Rogan. I'm quite capable of looking after myself. I have since I was eighteen." *Don't mistake me for your wife.*

"You think I'm putting you in the same bracket as Darby," he said, as if Lee's thoughts had been pinned to her collar. "You can't be more wrong. You and my wife… You're polar points apart."

"That's good to know because this situation, *my* situation is not your problem, nor—" she paused for emphasis "—is it up for discussion."

He remained on the couch, gaze steady, mouth somber and she thought again how unexpected his features were for a man toiling in an office and a courtroom. No smooth lawyerly looks, just hard edges and tough angles—the kind you'd imagine on a sawmill worker.

The kind that spiked her temperature.

So different from Stuart who had a choirboy's face, one that would age long after most of the population, including Lee. And although Oliver in a way resembled Rogan, gray-eyed and rough-featured, he had been more friend than lover. She'd never felt for Oliver—or Stuart, for that matter—what she wanted with Rogan.

"Okay," he said. "I respect your decision. But I won't be going away, Lee." He got to his feet, came to where she stood. "My guess is the father of your baby is out of the picture, or you wouldn't have kissed me. Which, in my books, makes you unattached." He touched her lips with his thumb. "Come for dinner. Danny and I will be expecting you at six."

He turned and walked across the room to the door.

Before he pulled it open, she asked, "Are you only interested because you need a mother for your son?"

The question reverberated in the silence that followed.

God, Lee, why can't you keep your mouth shut? Why

do you always have to blurt your opinions like some judgmental shrew?

Slowly, Rogan pivoted around. His eyes flashed an unfamiliar emotion. Anger. "If I wanted a mother for my son, I'd hire a nanny. See you later."

The soft click of the door closing echoed like a shot.

Are you only interested because you need a mother for your son?

Damn it. How could she ask such a question after that kiss? Didn't she get that he was so *into* her? How could she doubt his intentions?

Hell. He wanted to barge back and kiss her silly just to prove his point.

His office phone rang and he crossed to his desk next to the window. He and Danny had spent two hours after school last Tuesday setting up the place after The Old Wood Store delivered the furniture. Now the room looked exactly how Rogan pictured a small-town law office to be: L-shaped desk with computer, filing system, bulletin board and shelving for law books and case binders.

On a sigh, he checked caller ID. An alien number. "Hello."

"Mr. Matteo?" a man's voice asked.

Rogan yanked his emotions into place. "Speaking," he said pleasantly.

"Peyton Sawyer. I saw your sign yesterday. Didn't know you were opening your office so soon."

"What can I do for you, Mr. Sawyer?" Rogan walked around the desk's chair, flipped open a legal pad.

"I was talking to your brother a few weeks back…"

Ah, yes. The Desert Storm veteran Johnny mentioned last week.

The man had gone from flying fighter jets to flying Alaskan bush planes. And now he required assistance with his disability pension.

Rogan reached for a pen. "Are you still a licensed pilot, Mr. Sawyer?"

"I'm a pilot-for-hire. Fly Lee Tait's plane off and on."

He did? Lee hadn't mentioned the man.

After a lengthy discussion and copious notes, Rogan scheduled a meeting next Wednesday. Meanwhile, he'd do some digging with the Veterans Affairs Department. Hanging up the phone, he sat back. His first case as the island's only lawyer. Okay, he was taking the case *pro bono*—his rule for vets—but Peyton Sawyer would spread the word that Rogan's office was open for business.

He was half out of his chair to tell Lee that he'd just taken on his first client when he stopped. Because she lived two steps across a stairwell landing from his office did not mean she wanted him interfering in her life every minute of the day.

Besides, if he was to cook her dinner tonight he needed to visit Dalton Foods for some fresh produce and meat.

Fetching his suit jacket off the coat tree by the door, he headed for the rear entrance and his car. He'd buy a box of crackers and some ginger ale, as well. In case. They'd worked for Darby's first trimester; he hoped they'd work magic for Lee, too. And she would see he wasn't about to turn tail and run over her announcement.

Because that's what it was, now that he had time to analyze the last hour. She was scared he'd walk, so she'd made up her mind to walk first. Didn't take a genius to analyze her parting remark.

Well, Lee, he thought. *I don't know what your baby's father did to you. But I'm not him. And I'm here to stay.*

If only as a friend. If that's what she wanted. He hoped not.

Because, damn it, he wanted to kiss her again. He wanted to touch her hair. Feel her skin go damp and hot. Listen to her breathing hurry…

Jeez, Rogan, the woman is pregnant, for God's sake! Come October she'll be having another man's child.

Okay, he needed to focus on buying groceries for tonight. Carrots, salad, corn, broccoli—

Filing a lengthy mental list in order to keep Lee at bay, he went down the stairs two at a time.

Chapter Eight

In the mirror, Lee saw a woman dressed to please a man—
and to apologize for the way she had behaved earlier in
the day, after he'd laid out his heart about his tragedy.

She wore a black knit top that hugged her breasts and
an emerald wraparound skirt, which clung to her hips and
flowed against her legs like a small jungle waterfall.

The moment she parked in front of his big, rambling
farmhouse and Rogan came to help her descend from
the Jeep, she noticed the way his eyes darkened when
the skirt rippled in the sea breeze and drifted against his
knees. Then, as he made spaghetti and meatballs in his
lovely country kitchen, she caught his gaze. And again
during dinner with his son grinning across the table.

Dusk hadn't quite settled when Lee lowered herself
to the wooden glider he'd hung from a strong limb of

the century-aged Garry oak. She watched Rogan turn on the quaint lanterns strung along the porch eaves before he went back inside to fetch a blanket.

"How you feeling?" he asked, mantling her against the evening chill before he settled beside her.

"So far so good." She lifted the glass of ginger ale she'd brought from the dinner table.

His smile made her pulse thrum. "Never thought I'd be sitting out here on a balmy spring evening with a beautiful woman a week after moving in."

While he looked across the yard where Danny stood at the fence watching the horses graze, she studied the profile of the man beside her: his strong nose, the masculine slash of his mouth, his wide brow. Straight and black, his hair was neatly trimmed, yet it retained a length she could thread her fingers through—if she took a mind.

Pulling her gaze back to the glass in her hand, she said, "I want to apologize for my idiocy this afternoon. For the mothering comment." Shame washed through her at the memory. "Especially after everything you told me."

His head turned. "Truth is, I should be apologizing for doing the caveman chest thump when you weren't feeling well."

"Well." Her lips twitched. "It was a tad Neanderthal."

Leaning back, he set his arm along the back of the bench and she caught her breath. "You make me want to shout and dance and do dumb things. You make me feel again, Lee."

Lord, he'd taken her capacity to speak.

Discomfort flushed her skin. She had to tell him. Had to tell him she'd flown for Abner Air. That the company once owned the seaplane she now piloted, the seaplane he'd flown in several times. Most of all, she had to tell him it was her ex-husband he was suing.

Rogan drew closer. She knew he wanted to kiss her, so she let him. In this moment, on this glider, shadowed by the tree's sweeping branches, she heard the hum of evening approach. She did not want to think about Stuart and his company, or *that pilot* and what might have caused a plane to go down three years ago. Instead, she let Rogan cup her face, let his mouth cover hers, let herself sink into the sensation that only he elicited.

"Lee," he whispered, setting his forehead to hers a little while later. "I haven't felt this good in a long while." Inching away, he traced a fingertip slowly along her hairline, igniting a trail of tiny sparklers along the way.

Oh, how she longed to fall into the softness of his eyes, the kindness of his touch. "Rogan, I need to tell you s—"

A shriek pierced the air.

Instantly, Rogan was on his feet. "Danny."

Flinging the blanket aside, Lee jumped off the glider, searching the twilight where they had seen the boy moments ago at the fence, and where only emptiness greeted them. The horses had disappeared.

Danny cried again, and Rogan began running for the barn. "I'm coming, son!"

Rushing across the yard as fast as she could in the stilettos she'd worn, a single thought whipped through Lee's mind. *He's been through enough.*

"Daddy! Help me!" The boy's muffled voice came from inside the barn.

Oh, God. What had happened? Lee wondered, watching his father's broad back vanish beyond the entry doors.

Pictures of the building's run-down stalls rose up. Although the barn appeared structurally sound during her first visit, she had noted deterioration in several areas: the stall floorboards, the rusted hinges of the rear doors, and the slanted nesting cubicles in the chicken pen.

"Where are you, son?" Rogan called.

Darkness cloaked the interior and it took several seconds for Lee's eyes to adjust before the sea-gray shirt Rogan had donned for dinner came into focus.

"Up here, Daddy."

"There," Lee said, pointing to where the child's leg dangled from a fracture in the ceiling above a rear horse stall.

Rogan strode forward. "I see you." Panic rode his voice at the sight of Danny trapped in the jagged hole; Lee swallowed back her own dread. "Hang on, buddy," his father soothed. "I'm here."

"A board broke and I fell, Daddy. Can you come up and get me? I'm scared."

Lee caught Rogan's arm before he scrambled up the rickety ladder nailed to the wall above the manger. The ladder led to a narrow rectangular opening used for tossing down hay and straw from the loft. "I'll go. You'll be too heavy."

His eyes snapped with conflict, and she understood. She was pregnant. She shouldn't be climbing into haylofts.

"I'm fine, Rogan," she assured before he could protest. "I've been jogging up and down hills and through wooded trails for three years. A ten-foot ladder is nothing. Besides, we really don't have a choice. You need to stay here. In case…"

In case Danny falls through.

His eyes wove up to his child. "It's not safe," he muttered. He scanned her dress, the pointy heels. "It's not safe," he repeated.

She laid her hand against his cheek. "It'll be okay. Trust me. I've climbed up there hundreds of times." *Yes, as a kid, Lee. Not as a pregnant adult.* She kept that tidbit to herself.

"I owe you," he said, his eyes clinging to hers.

"You owe me nothing, except to stay right here. Danny," she called, turning for the ladder. "I'm coming up to get you."

"I want my Daddy." Tears choked the boy's words.

"I know, honey, but Daddy needs to stay under you. He's the only one strong enough to catch you if you fall through. Okay?" *Make the situation perfectly clear,* she thought.

"Okay."

Eight days ago, when she walked through the barn to see Rogan and Danny paint, the ladder's structure hadn't registered. She'd been too intent on Rogan to remember clambering with her friend Eve up a ladder nailed to a wall.

A ladder that today missed a couple of rungs.

Removing her heels to stand in panty hose, Lee stared up at the dark square hole in line with the manger.

How had the boy gotten up there? *The same way I did at ten.* She threw Rogan one more glance. "You'll be fine," she said, and grabbed a rung, tested its reliability.

Cautiously she made her way upward.

"Hey, guy," she said, popping above the floor of the loft. The child sat ten feet inside, one leg curled under him, while the other vanished into the ragged hole.

"Will I fall, Ms. Tait?"

"No, honey. But we will need to be careful. Now, I want you to lie down and stretch your hands to mine."

From where she balanced on the second highest rung, Lee reached across the floor. The boy's grip was firm, his palms sweaty.

With gentle persuasion she coaxed him to draw his leg from the fissure and inch his way toward the loft opening.

Lee blew a long, quiet breath when she finally tugged him to the edge of the entrance and safety.

Rogan stood below them, in the stall. "Danny, let Lee climb down so I can come up and piggyback you down."

"I'm not scared anymore, Dad. I can do it."

"All right, pal." Rogan held out his hands. "I've got you. Just come down nice and easy."

A minute later, the boy stood securely in the stall and while Lee slipped on her heels, Rogan checked his child for bruises and scrapes.

"Why did you go up there, Daniel?" he asked, his tone no longer panicked.

Danny nudged a lump of dirt with the toe of his sneaker. "Pepper was galloping around an' then the horses went over the hill and—and I couldn't see 'em anymore."

"So you decided to climb up in the loft when I told you specifically to never go up there?"

"I'm sorry, Dad."

Sighing, Rogan bent down on one knee. Scraping at his hair, he said, "You scared me silly, know that?"

"I didn't mean to." The boy's lip quivered. "I just wanted to see the horses."

"What if you really had fallen?"

"I'd be hurt?"

"Or worse."

Lee watched Rogan's Adam's apple bob as he pulled his son into a hug. "I need you to listen to me, Danny," he said and his eyes told Lee of possible nightmares. Danny broken and bleeding on the barn floor. Danny in the hospital. Danny in a coma. Danny…

Don't think it, Rogan. "He's okay," she whispered. *You're okay.*

He got to his feet, looked down at the boy. "Dan, you know when you don't listen there are consequences."

"Yeah…"

"Tonight you'll go to bed early."

"But, Dad, it's Friday," the boy complained, fear of the ordeal vanishing in a blink. "I get to stay up till nine-thirty on Fridays."

"Not this Friday."

"Aw…"

"Not another word, Daniel."

Bottom lip poking out, the boy turned and headed out of the barn. Suddenly, he ran back and hugged Lee around the waist. "Thanks for saving me," he whispered.

She ran a hand over his silky hair. "You're welcome, Dan."

After he left the barn again, she drew a deep sigh. "Your son is going to break hearts one day, Rogan."

"If I teach him right, he won't. He'll treat a woman with respect and integrity."

"Did you at sixteen?" she teased.

A half laugh exploded. "I hope so. Though I admit, I wasn't always interested in a woman's mind at the time. Here, let me brush the hay off your skirt." His hand whispered across her lap and knees, and her breath caught. "There," he said. His eyes were dark as a Pacific storm, and for a second she believed he'd kiss her. Instead, he said, "Let's go back."

They walked across the yard. Danny mounted the porch steps, dragging the ball and chain of consequence. Her heart reached out. "Aren't you being a little hard on him with the early bedtime?"

"I can't take the chance he'll disobey me at every turn. His life depends on it here."

"Here? Rogan, he climbed into a hayloft, not down a well. Kids get into problem situations in a city, too."

"A board broke," he said, not hearing her. "It could've been his neck. I would think you'd see my side in this."

"I do see it." She paused by the oak where minutes before they had kissed. On the porch Danny shot his father a last dejected look before entering the house. The door closed softly behind him.

Letting his head fall back, Rogan blew a hefty sigh. "Do you know he literally stopped my heart?"

"Nope," Lee chided, setting a palm against his chest. "Still strong and steady."

He pulled her into his arms. "If it hadn't been for you..." His body shuddered, effects from the aftermath. She wrapped her arms around him.

"Hush," she soothed. "It all turned out fine."

He didn't answer. Rather, his mouth found hers in a crushing kiss that spoke of the fear he bottled inside, of the tragedy he still suffered. His tongue vaulted around hers. Hard, passionate, the kiss streamed heat into every nerve ending.

Rogan, was all she could think. If he wanted to take her right there, she would let him.

Abruptly, he wrenched free and stared down at her. "Lee, I'm sorry. I don't know what I was thinking treating you like some kind of—" Driving his hands into his hair, he put three steps between them. "It's this place. I shouldn't have bought it. Danny could've— A farm is no place for a city kid. I should've stayed in Renton."

Lee gazed at the man who just kissed off her lips, whose shoulders hunched against the weight of his decisions. She wanted to say, *It's not the farm that's the problem.*

"I suppose," she said slowly, "your best option would be to sell it. To run away…again." Although he hadn't explained his reasoning in so many words, her woman's intuition said he'd come to Firewood Island to do exactly that. Flee.

He reeled around, his brows battering rams, his eyes beneath them cold. "You know nothing about it."

It. His sorrow. His demon.

She lifted her chin. "The father of my baby is dead, Rogan. He was killed in Iraq by sniper fire. So, yes, I *do* know something about it." *We might have only been friends with benefits, but I still miss him.*

His gaze flicked to her stomach where her hands had gone to protect, and instantly the fight in him dissolved. She saw it in the tilt of his head, heard it in the sigh along his lips. "Lee, I'm…"

She shook her head. "Regrets are useless. The past is done and gone. All that matters is what you decide, here and now." She walked to her vehicle.

"Where you going?"

"Home." Climbing behind the wheel, she said, "Say goodnight to Danny for me." Then she started the engine—and left him to his choices.

* * *

A solemn quiet greeted Rogan when he entered the house. After she'd driven away, he paced a rut on the porch. *Regrets are useless.* Naturally, she was right. He needed to get over his fear of unforeseen tragedies happening to Danny. But, God, it was hard. The boy was all he had left. All he lived for.

Selling the farm would break his son's heart. The kid was crazy about the horses; they were the reason he climbed into the loft in the first place. *And the reason he'd almost injured himself.*

Ruthlessly, Rogan sliced off the thought. Accidents happened. Hell, since his toddler days he'd heard the tired example, "walking across the street could kill you." As an adult and a lawyer, he understood that kind of fate. Crud happened. Everywhere. To anyone.

Living here wasn't a guarantee for safety. It was a choice, one he wanted to believe was as good as any he had made in his life.

All that matters is what you decide, here and now.

With Lee's words circling his mind, he took the stairs to the upper floor and Danny's bedroom.

"Hey, bud," he said, pausing on the threshold.

The boy wore his superhero pj's and his hair lay damp on his forehead from washing his face. "Do I really have to go to bed, Dad?"

Aren't you being a little hard on him? Her words again.

Damn it, she was right; sending a seven-year-old to bed at 7:35 on a Friday night for climbing into a barn loft was a tad harsh.

"Maybe we can compromise," Rogan said.

"What's compr'ise?"

"Com-*pro*-mise. It means we find a solution that suits us both."

Danny fidgeted with the sheet. "'Kay."

"So. What do you think is a fair consequence for not listening?"

The child shrugged a bony shoulder. "I dunno. I don't get to play with my digger?"

Rogan hid a smile. The boy loved the digger Lee had given him. "Sounds like a good one. All right. It's mine for the weekend."

His son debated the lost fun hours. Mournful eyes looked up. "All weekend?"

"Until Monday. Seal the deal?" Rogan held out a hand, his heart tugging when his son bumped knuckles. Pulling Danny into a quick hug, he said, "And we won't talk about this anymore, all right?"

"'Kay."

"Want to watch the movie I brought home this afternoon?"

"With Ms. Tait?"

"Lee had to go home."

"Aw…"

Rogan brushed the hair from his son's eyes. "You like her, don't you, son?"

"Yeah. She's cool. Will she come back to see us?"

"I hope so."

Danny climbed out of bed, sat on the mat to pull on a pair of heavy socks. "She told me when she was little she built a road with a bridge in her mom's flowerbed. Isn't that cool, Dad? I never knew a girl who liked playing in the dirt."

"Me, neither, bud." But he could see Lee doing

exactly that. He pictured those big green eyes lit with a child's delight; a smudge on her freckled cheek; finger-nails limned with rich, moist earth.

Downstairs he slid the disc into the player, started the movie. While the trailers played, he made popcorn; then once he had Danny settled on the sofa, he returned to the kitchen and called Lee.

He hadn't been able to get her out of his mind, and certainly not after she mentioned the father of her baby. Rogan wondered when the man had died. At the most a couple of months ago. A very short time. Had he known she was pregnant? Had she loved him?

Damn. She had suffered the man's death, and con-tinued to suffer. Tonight he'd seen it in her eyes.

And how had he treated her? *As a self-absorbed jerk, a complete jackass.*

The phone was on its sixth ring. She hadn't returned home—or she wasn't answering.

Her machine clicked on.

"Lee," he said, his throat aching. "If you're there, please pick up. I…" His fingers cleaved through his hair. "I'm sorry for acting like a barbarian after what you did for Dan. Can I make it up to you, take you to dinner or lunch or breakfast—or, hell, why not make it all three?" His attempt at humor failed. "Okay," he said when she still hadn't picked up. "I'll let you decide. Talk to you later."

He wanted to say *soon. Talk to you soon.* Better yet, *Now.*

With a sigh, he set down the receiver. Truth was, he shouldn't have called at all—or left that dumbass message. Apologies should be said in person. The last time he left a message on Darby's voicemail had been the morning he watched her and Sophie get in a taxi bound for the airport. And he'd gone to work.

She'd never picked up the call, never heard his *We'll get through this, Dar. We will.*

By the time he'd gathered the day's documents, statements and depositions off his desk for his 10:00 a.m. schedule in court, she and their daughter were dead.

These days, leaving a voicemail kicked his pulse into overdrive—more so when the recipient was someone he cared for, and especially if he wasn't sure she would get the message. *Nothing's wrong. She's just gone to visit one of her sisters.* He hoped.

Kneading the nape of his neck, he returned to the living room and his son.

She listened to his voice on the answering machine, but remained on the couch, sipping a cup of blackberry tea. Strings of clear, mini lights lit the wharf, adding a silvery sheen to the dark water lapping beneath. To the far left, she saw the white outline of her plane's wing in the amber glow of a lamppost. To the right, down another jut, Lu's Foot Ferry was anchored for the night.

When the machine shut off, she got up and pressed Play and once more let his voice sink into her senses.

She wanted to accept his apology. She wanted to call back, say, *I understand.* That when life punches you sideways, it takes a bit to find your footing again.

She remembered the hunger of his kiss after the loft dilemma, the hot emotions. She knew she should forget him, end their relationship, such as it was. She did not need a man riding the coattails of heartbreak and, God forbid, the trouble her previous association with Abner Air would provoke.

Still, she reached for the telephone—and withdrew. Somewhere along the way, Rogan had become important to her. Deep down important. She wanted their relationship to survive.

But how? When she told him who she was... It would be over. She wouldn't need to end it, *he'd* do it for her. In a heartbeat.

Lifting the receiver, she punched Kat's number. Her sister would know what to do, and so would Addie, except she and Skip had plans tonight. It was Friday, after all.

"What's up, Lee?" Kat asked the instant she picked up. "Everything okay?"

Her sister sensing Lee's turmoil hit a nerve. She burst into tears. "Oh, Kat...I don't know what to dooo..."

"Hey, hey," Kat consoled. "I'm here, honey. Take in a deep breath."

Lee tried, and instead gulped and sobbed harder.

"What is it?" Kat asked, genuine concern in her tone. "Is it the baby?"

"No," Lee choked. *"Yes."*

"I'll be there in two minutes."

"No, no," Lee said quickly. "The baby's fine. It's— It's everything on top of the baby. Rogan, Oliver, Sky Dash." She swiped at her tears, pulled the afghan over her and curled into a fetal position on the couch. God, she was a mess. "And once I start showing, the whispers will start. Oh, Kat, my life's a photocopy of Mom's. Ex-husband, illicit affair, and onto guy number three."

"Okay, let's deal with the Mom thing first. Will you keep Oliver's name a secret from the baby?"

The way Charmaine had with Kat. To this day, Lee's sister didn't know the name of her biological father. *Mom's closet secret,* as the sisters referred to Charmaine's refusal to speak of the man, had elicited myriad arguments over the years.

Lee sniffed and wiped her tears. "The second this child is born it'll know who Oliver Duvall was, and that I loved him." *In a good and decent way, and as a true friend.*

"There you go," Kat said. "You're not Mom. I love her and all, but this thing between her and me... But never mind that. Let's talk about Oliver."

"I'm so ashamed." Lee sniffed.

"Why?"

"Because people mourning their lover's death shouldn't feel all hormonal about another man a couple months later."

"Okay, slow down. You said you loved Oliver. We know that. He was your closest childhood friend. But were you *in* love with him?"

Thumbing away her tears, Lee sighed. "Truth? I'm not sure. We were two lonely adults who'd known each other forever and simply took that relationship to the next level one night. Sure, we talked marriage afterward, but it was more a comfort idea. But with Rogan... Oh, Kat, I've never felt like this. He's..." She pinched the bridge of her nose. "God, I can't stop thinking about him. And I...I shouldn't. He's got so many issues, never mind that his wife and daughter were passengers on that plane Stuart lost three years ago."

"Are you serious?"

"I wish I weren't."

"Does he know?"

"That I'm Stuart's ex-wife, and flew for Abner Air? No. But it won't be long before he finds out. He's been assembling a case against Stuart for three years."

"Are you saying you and Stuart were still married when—"

"No. I'm saying I used to fly *that* plane, Kat. When it went down, I called his office to convey my condolences and the secretary told me then which plane they'd lost. It was one *I'd* always flown." *The one Stuart let Bill Norton fly.*

"Oh, Lee…"

"A mess, huh? And don't forget, my Sky Dash was once part of Stuart's fleet."

Several beats of silence hovered. Kat said, "You weren't to blame, Lee. There were dozens of rumors back then about why the crash happened. I don't remember them all, but I do remember talk of a faulty fuel gage, a storm, even pilot error."

"Bill Norton," Lee said, zeroing on the man in the cockpit that day. "He took my place. If I hadn't—"

"Hadn't what? Divorced Stuart? He cheated on you, Lee. Have you forgotten that?"

A vision of Stuart in *their* bed with that cocktail waitress could still make Lee's stomach churn. "No," she whispered.

"Listen," Kat went on. "You are an excellent pilot. But you need to tell Rogan. If you want a relationship with this man, you need to be up front about this part of your past. And don't leave anything out."

"He'll never speak to me again."

"Then he isn't the one."

The finality of Kat's words haunted Lee into the weekend.

Chapter Nine

Early Saturday, she flew three family members to a Whidbey Island reunion before returning to jog the shoreline trail alone. Kat couldn't come because her son had an earache, and Addie was following Skip's wishes to walk her miles on the treadmill at home.

Exhilarated and sweaty from her run, Lee opened the door of her apartment to a ringing phone. Her next flight—a pair of newlyweds wanting a tour of the island and Admiralty Inlet—wouldn't be until 3:00 p.m.

"How'd your run go?" Addie asked without preamble.

"Great. Yours?"

"Not as good as breathing the sea wind, but it makes Skip more comfortable to have me at home."

Lee understood Skip's concern and envied his

devotion to Addie. The man displayed attributes Lee had not experienced in her own marriage. And although her relationship with Oliver had been lovely and strong, she realized now that she hadn't loved him with that all-out passion she saw between Addie and Skip. While some might call it coveting, Lee wanted what they had—and she wanted it with Rogan.

Pushing the thought aside, she said, "You exercising at home makes me happier, too, Ads. You shouldn't be somewhere in the woods at this stage of the game."

"Yeah," her sister conceded. "I know. Listen, have you told Mom about the baby?"

"Not yet." That was another added worry. Her mother's reaction. Lee didn't look forward to Charmaine Wilson's I-expected-more-of-you remarks.

"Don't leave it till later," Addie went on. "All things considered, she does have a right to know, never mind that she'd be really hurt if you waited until you show."

"I don't need her condescending attitude right now."

"She's changed."

"Maybe for you."

Addie was silent. Then she asked the clincher. "What if you didn't tell her and something were to happen?"

Lee thought of Darby's plane, of Oliver in Iraq. "Fine. Soon as I shower I'll give her a call."

"Not call. Go over to the house."

The one with a million childhood memories—some not so good. Lee winced. "All right, I'll go," she said.

Thirty minutes later, she turned her SUV into Charmaine Wilson's dirt lane on the outskirts of town. The tiny six-room Cape Cod-style home, surrounded by evergreens, oaks and maples, put a lump into Lee's throat. She'd always loved this house. And yes, she loved her mother. She just wished they got along better.

At her first knock, Charmaine swung open the door. "Lee. What a nice surprise."

"Hi, Mom."

"Come on in." Her mother stepped back as Lee entered. The scent of butter and sugar hung on the air. On days Charmaine didn't cut hair at the Looks Good salon, she baked for her daughters' families.

"Which kind did you make today?" Lee wanted to know. She'd never been able to refuse her mother's treats.

"Your favorite," Charmaine said.

Lee went through the house to the kitchen. "Carrot cake?"

"You want a piece?" Her mother got the kettle to make tea.

"A small slice. Mom—" Lee walked to the window that looked out on the backyard. Purple crocuses decorated the dark flowerbeds. "I'm pregnant."

Charmaine set the kettle down. "You're...?"

"The baby is Oliver Duvall's and it's due late October."

Her mother sat down at the kitchen table. "But before...you weren't able to..."

Lee shrugged. "Guess Stuart was useless in more ways than one."

"Oh, Lee." Elbows on the table, Charmaine cupped her cheeks. "How on Earth did you get in this position?"

She laughed without humor. "Position?"

Her mother sat back, eyes penetrating. "I meant how did you *allow* yourself—"

Lee held up her hands and walked to the kitchen doorway. "Do not go there, Mother. The last thing I need is your judgment." Why had she come? She shouldn't have come. Or she should have brought Addie to act as a buffer.

Charmaine rushed after Lee to the front door. "I'm not judgmental, I'm worried. How will you run Sky Dash?"

"I don't know. Maybe Peyton Sawyer will buy it. He's always wanted full-time work." If it meant he wouldn't have to move his family off the island.

"The retired bush pilot? You don't want that."

In the foyer, Lee turned. "First off, Mom, he's an excellent pilot and second, it's not a matter of wanting. It's a matter of necessity." She pushed out the door and strode to her vehicle. "I'll see you later."

"Lee, darn it." Charmaine hurried down the stoop. "Let's talk this over."

"We have. You're not happy with my behavior, but you know what? You'll just have to deal with it somehow." She yanked open the truck's door, jumped behind the wheel. Why had she expected her mother's support?

"What about Lucien Duvall? Have you told him?"

Lee's hand stalled on the ignition. "I'll go there now." *Might as well get it out now as later.*

Her mother stepped into the yawning door. "Would you like me to come along?" Her eyes were as serious as Lee had seen. "He's… He's not an easy man."

Lee laughed and the tension left her shoulders. "No kidding."

"I won't say a word," her mother persisted. "I'll just be there. For you."

Lee struggled with the decision. Should she take the olive branch? "Thanks," she said, offering a small smile.

"But I need to do this on my own. He might think we're ganging up on him."

Charmaine looked down the driveway. "It wouldn't be the first time," she murmured.

Lee frowned. "Meaning…?"

The older woman stepped back. "Call me when you're home."

"Sure." She turned the engine, pressed the accelerator and drove from her childhood home. As always she wondered why she let her mother get to her.

Lucien Duvall lived in a houseboat on the other side of Burnt Bend, along the only river that ran half the length of the island. When Mrs. Duvall had died of cancer the year Oliver graduated from Fire High, the old man sold their house in town, bought the houseboat, and Oliver left to make the military his career.

His old pickup and Oliver's black SUV were parked in the small graveled spot in front of the houseboat. Lee felt the sting of tears at the sight of Oliver's truck. Lucien hadn't sold it yet.

As she got out of her vehicle, he glanced up from his task on the houseboat's small, square deck. She recalled their last meeting at her apartment; a shiver ran up her spine. *The Duvall* was moored several hundred yards upstream from the cluster of other houseboats sharing this section of river beach.

"Hello, Lucien," she said.

"Whaddya want?"

"I'd like to talk to you for a minute. Do you mind if I come aboard?"

"Suit yourself."

She went across the short gangplank and stepped onto the deck. Dressed in jeans, boots and a thick winter vest against the cool April weather, the old man sat on a patio chair, carving wood. A breeze caught his silver hair, tufting it at the back of his head.

Lee stood watching his big hands, the knife between them. On a deep breath, she said, "I'm pregnant with Oliver's child, Lucien."

He gave her a sideways glance. "I'm supposed to believe that?"

"I don't care if you do or don't. I'm telling you so there won't be any surprises when the baby's born." After all, people around town had seen her holding Oliver's hand.

He grunted, continued to carve. "Nothing you or your mother does surprises me."

She stood for a moment longer, fascinated how he groomed the wood in the shape of a woman holding a cat.

"Well," Lee said, chilled by his indifference. "I'll leave you to your carving."

She was almost at the Jeep when his gruff voice rang out. "You'll call me when the baby's born?" He stood at the deck railing, gazing down at her, hands at his sides clutching wood and knife. An imposing bear of a man, he looked vulnerable against the day's sunshine.

A slow smile crossed Lee's lips. "I will. You take care, Lucien."

Her visits with Charmaine and Lucien intensified Lee's thoughts of Rogan. There was obviously a history between her mother and Lucien. Both had made vague references to the other, and then both opted not to elaborate. And Lee's instincts told her that history occurred decades before—and continued, unresolved.

She would not repeat the same process with Rogan.

Kat's right, she thought Monday morning as she and Fitz loaded the seaplane. *I should've informed him immediately about my association with Abner Air.*

The instant Rogan explained the basis for his anxiety as they flew back to Burnt Bend, she should have opened her mouth and told him of *her* past. If she had, she wouldn't be in this state today, harboring knowledge akin to some sort of terrible secret.

Secret. How she hated the word. Well, after returning from this morning's flight, she would knock on his office door and tell him. Just walk in and spill it all.

Since their confrontation Friday evening, he'd left voicemails for her to call him, the third message coming at nine last night. Each Lee saved—and listened to again and again.

She'd needed time to think. Kat and Addie would call it *picking the problem apart,* and they'd be right. She'd always been one to analyze situations to death. Like the night she had dinner with Kat, questioning her sister about Rogan. And what about the other night over the phone? No, that night she'd fallen apart.

She never cried. But that night…

Something had snapped.

"That's it," Fitz said, interrupting her worries as he slammed the cargo hold closed. "See ya at four, girl."

"Thanks, Fitz." Lee watched him pull the trolley down the dock. In the two weeks he'd been loading her plane, he hadn't once asked why she needed his help.

He'd simply accepted her request—and her privacy. But that wasn't why she'd gone to him. Fitz and his wife ran Coffee Sense, and Lee had known the couple from the time she was sixteen and worked her first after-school job in their shop. In those days Fitz became the surrogate father she'd needed.

After climbing into the plane, she tugged the door shut. Time to concentrate on the flight....

Two hours later, she taxied back to the dock and anchored the plane. Glancing toward the shops, she wondered if Rogan had heard her approach. Was he watching out the window?

He hadn't flown with her today, which meant he was probably at his desk. A knot seizing her stomach, Lee headed for the building.

At the top of the staircase, she knocked on his door with its gold nameplate, Rogan B. Matteo, Attorney, bolted at eye level, a nameplate that hadn't been there this morning.

"Come in, Lee," he called.

So he had been watching for her.

"Hey," she said, entering.

He was alone, but rose immediately to come around his desk. Eyes dark and serious, he said, "I thought you'd left the island. I tried to call several times."

"I'm sorry, it was a busy weekend." Guilt seared her cheeks. "Rogan, I need to tell you about—"

He reached for her hands. "When you didn't answer your phone last night, I thought I'd really pissed you off."

"No. I was just…" *Trying to figure out how to tell you about my marriage to Stuart and everything that involved.* "Busy. And last night," she added hurriedly because "busy" sounded arrogant, "I wasn't up to talking, so I went to bed early."

He studied her for a moment, then touched her cheek. "You were exhausted."

"A little tired. Okay, more than a little." She laughed softly. "Goes with the territory, I suppose."

"Are you free for a while?"

"Actually, I need to do some paperwork, but first we need to—"

"It can wait. Come." He steered her toward the door, his hand warm and gentle on her waist. "I'll brew a pot of your favorite tea while you rest on the sofa."

"That isn't necessary." But, Lord, it sounded wonderful. In her mind, a picture flashed: them together, her head in his lap while he stroked her hair, her falling into a deep and restful sleep.

He locked his office while she unlocked her apartment.

"Hang on," she said, suddenly realizing her bladder was about to burst.

Rogan nodded. "I'll get the water boiling."

In the bathroom mirror, Lee stared at the dark circles under her eyes. *He understands,* she thought, touching skin the color of an eggplant. *He knows what a pregnant woman goes through.* And there they were again, the tears.

Disgusted with herself, she ran the washcloth under cold water, patted her face. *Pull yourself together. This is so not you.*

She finished her business and was walking into the kitchen when the cramp hit. "Oooh," she cried softly, grasping the back of a chair and her stomach at the same time.

Rogan's head snapped around. Immediately, he set the kettle down and strode over. His pupils pinpointed. "What is it?" he asked, his arm warm and steady around her hunched shoulders.

"Got a…pain…in my…stomach."

Pulling out the chair, he guided Lee onto it. Squatting in front of her, he coaxed, "Slow, deep breaths."

Sharp and keen, the pain lanced again across her abdomen. Lee doubled over. Her face nearly touched her knees. "Rogan…" she panted. "The baby…I won't let it…" *Go.*

He tore the cell phone off his belt. "I'm calling 9-1-1."

Lee grabbed his hand. "Wait— It's—It's lessening." And it was. A little. She shut her eyes, panted. "I'm okay, now."

"Lee, you can't even sit straight."

Breathing through her mouth, she remained curled over her knees. Gradually, the pain ebbed. Within a minute, it disappeared altogether. She sat back with a sigh. "Must have been something I ate this morning."

"I don't like it," Rogan said, his gaze troubled. "I think you should see a doctor."

"Did Darby have cramps?"

"No, but with Danny she spotted in her third trimester. Turned out to be marginal placenta previa."

Rogan glanced toward the bathroom. "Are you…?"

Spotting. "No. But the doctor said if it does happen I should get to a clinic right away. Not that something is wrong, but she'd rather not take the chance at this stage."

His eyes held hers. "Even so, I think you should go to the clinic, Lee."

She wasn't a fool. She had a dozen things against her, most significantly her age and the fact this would be her first child. "Okay," she whispered.

Rogan helped her from the chair. "I'll drive you."

Gingerly, Lee straightened her spine. "I'm not an invalid, Rogan."

"Humor me."

"What about your work? You've just opened your business."

"And this is your first baby."

She slanted him a look. "How would you know?"

He swiped her keys off the counter and walked her to the rear door of the apartment. "I just know."

"Is that a lawyer thing, this just knowing?"

Before he ushered her slowly out onto the back staircase, he kissed her forehead. "It's because I know *you.*"

Lee sputtered a laugh. "What? Two and a half weeks gives us a history?"

"Ever hear of déjà vu?"

Her heart echoed his words. "Don't play games, Rogan," she stated, heading down the stairs. "I'm not in the mood."

At the bottom, he caught her arm, turned her gently around. Sunshine squinted his eyes, magnified their dense lashes.

"No game, Lee. I feel something for you. There's a connection between us. A connection I haven't felt in a helluva long time. Don't ask how it happened so fast. It just did."

Opening the passenger door of the truck, he helped her inside, before walking around the hood, jingling the keys in his hand—and all she could do was stare at him through the windshield.

If she had any doubts about their relationship, they slammed against her heart the moment he uttered the words.

Déjà vu.

Connection.

In her case, they could be one and the same.

She'd felt it the instant he'd spoken to her that evening on the dock, an invisible thread linked one to the other, humming through her blood.

He slid behind the wheel, turned the ignition. Leaning across the console, he kissed her mouth. "You're important to me," he said, voice low and deep. "It's that simple."

And you to me. But she kept the thought to herself as he drove to Burnt Bend Medical. *Once this is over I'll explain the true déjà vu between us.* The thought had her clenching a fist against her stomach.

Rogan's wristwatch read two o'clock by the time the nurse came for Lee in the waiting room. He couldn't sit any longer. The instant she vanished down the narrow hallway, he headed outside to get some air and pace the small parking lot in front of the clinic.

Damn it, she would be okay. He had to keep telling himself that. But, God forbid, if something did happen…

Wrong direction, Rogan. Think positively. She's a strong woman, mentally, emotionally. Sure, she was a little weepy. Wasn't she entitled? Hell, she was pregnant;

her hormones were jouncing all over the map. But beyond that, beyond the child within her—or perhaps because of it—he knew there hovered a fierce determination.

He'd seen that determination emerge a dozen times. In the way she told him she could find her own way to the clinic. The way she climbed into a loft to save his boy. And what about the days she'd taken him into her tiny plane while acknowledging his nerves, his tension?

In each incident hadn't she told him all would be fine?

Still, he paced. And punched a hand through his hair as he glanced at the clinic doors. The pounding of his heart matched the rhythm of his boot heels thudding the asphalt.

She was okay.

And if not…it would be Nature saying *this is not right and cannot work.*

The door to the clinic opened and he spun around.

Keys in hand, Lucien Duvall stepped out. Their eyes met. Without a word, the old man headed for his two-toned pickup.

Over the course of his career, Rogan had learned to read people, to sense hundreds of personalities, behaviors and attitudes. Within a few minutes of chatting, he could peg whether they were honest or nervous or con artists or….

He couldn't peg Lucien Duvall.

In the waiting room, the old man had stared at Lee until the nurse called her name. At her apartment Duvall displayed the demeanor of a schoolyard bully. Today, Rogan sensed a deep and lonely ache inside the man.

Abruptly, the guy turned from the truck's door. Eyes

narrowed under grizzled brows, he said, "You're that new lawyer, ain't ya?"

"I've opened an office here, yes. It's above the coffee shop."

"I know where it is, Mr. Matteo."

Of course, the man would know Rogan's name. With a population of eight hundred, Burnt Bend had village status. Newcomers were hard to miss.

Duvall jerked his chin toward the door. "Saw you come in with Lee Tait. You datin' her?"

"I don't think that's your business, Mr. Duvall."

The old man grunted. "Figured."

The door opened again and Lee stepped outside, a slip of paper in hand. She shot Rogan a look, then to his amazement she smiled at Duvall, who stepped away from his truck.

Not liking the man's questions or behavior, Rogan moved to intercept him.

"Hello, Lucien," Lee said, approaching them both.

"You sick?" he asked.

"No, are you?"

Her quick response had him pursing his lips. "Thought I might've busted my arm," he said.

"Ouch."

His eyes drilled Lee. "Was putting Oliver's truck up on blocks and the jack slipped."

Rogan saw something change in Lee. It wasn't so much a physical change as a spiritual one. Slowly her head turned and her eyes searched his for a long moment. "Oliver," she said, "was Lucien's son…and a soldier."

Was.

Suddenly, everything clicked. This man was the father of her boyfriend—the one who died at the hands of a sniper.

Lucien Duvall was the grandfather of her baby.

Did he know? Rogan wondered. Was the baby the cause for the regret in the old guy's eyes?

Rogan wanted to whisk Lee away from this depressing spot, this man who seemed to pull his sorrow around him like a cloak.

"Lee." Rogan touched her arm. "We should go." *You need to lie down and rest.*

"Call me if you need anything, Lucien," she said softly.

"Huh." With that he got into his truck and slammed the door.

By the time Rogan helped Lee into his car Duvall had barreled out of the parking lot.

"Friendly guy," he said, starting the car. If Duvall had booted Lee aside, he couldn't have hurt her more.

She leaned back against the headrest. "Oliver is the father of my baby."

"I know."

She rolled her head to look at him. Her eyes arrowed one question: *How did you guess?*

Rogan drove onto the street. "It wasn't hard to figure out. What did the doctor say?"

"She thinks it could be stress, so she wants me—correction, she's ordered me to take the remainder of the week off, preferably to get pampered and waited on until I relax enough to sort through the maze that's my current life."

Looking at Lee, he agreed with the doctor's diagnosis. Tension radiated from her body. Her hands clenched her purse as she stared out the side window.

"How the heck do I take a week's vacation?" she muttered. "I'll lose my business."

"Who flies for you when you get the flu?"

"I don't get sick."

"Ah. Let me guess…you never take vacations, either." He couldn't suppress his cynicism. "This is for your baby, Lee."

"I know," she whispered, visibly sagging beneath his words. "But to answer your question, Peyton Sawyer flies Sky Dash when I have another commitment."

Rogan nodded. "I'll take you to one of your sisters."

"No, just take me to the apartment. Addie's almost due and Kat's busy with her B and B."

He didn't like the idea of her staying alone—not since he'd learned of her pregnancy. "Your mother then?"

A humorless laugh. "No, thanks. The last thing I need is to live under a microscope again." She gusted a weary sigh that traveled to the arches of his feet. "Just take me home."

"Thought you'd never ask."

"I meant *my* home, Rogan. Look, I'm perfectly capable of taking care of myself."

"Fine. Here's the deal," he said, trying to keep his hands light on the wheel. "The doctor said rest and relaxation. So I'll give you a choice. We go to your place, and Danny and I look after you there. Or you come to the farm."

"Oh, for heaven's sake. Women all over do this on their own."

"Not my woman," he grumbled.

She turned slowly. "Okay. You are going totally hairy-backed caveman on me."

At that he threw back his head and laughed. "I'll have you know I don't have a single noticeable hair on my back."

"Be serious."

"I am." At the intersection, he flicked the signal left—down Clover Road, to the elementary school. "But first we need to pick up Danny, then we'll go home."

"If you don't turn this car around right this minute, Rogan—"

He pulled to the shoulder and stopped. Rotating in his seat, he slipped his hand under her hair. "Look at me, Lee." When she did, he thought the green of her eyes might swallow him whole. "I'm excessively in like with you. Maybe even more." If he had the guts to be honest and lay it all out on the table, he'd admit he'd fallen in love with her.

"Rogan, I…you've…"

He set two fingers on her mouth. "Shhh. I don't expect anything in return. Only that you come home with me and let me look after you. Please."

She shook her head. "I can't. There are things you don't know, things I need to tell—"

"Lee, you can make arrangements for your courier service from my couch."

"Yes, but…" She pressed a palm to her forehead. "What about *your* work?"

"I can work from home. Besides, having both of us there will make Danny very happy." Okay, he was using leverage he shouldn't, but he wanted Lee with him. He wanted to be there for her the way he hadn't for Darby.

She leaned back against his hand, sighed. "Bringing some woman into your house is not a good idea."

"Not some woman. You. And Danny will think it's a great idea. The second you brought that toy digger, you hung his moon. Helping him down from the loft just cinched the deal." Rogan stroked a tendril of hair from her cheek. "Come home with me, Lee."

"Are you always this pushy?" she asked, resigned.

He kissed her temple. "Not pushy. Concerned." Putting the car in gear, he reentered the road. "You won't be sorry."

"That," she mumbled, "remains to be seen."

Rebuking the gloom of her statement, he drove the four blocks to Burnt Bend Elementary.

Sitting in one of the two cushioned rocking chairs on Rogan's porch, Lee called Peyton Sawyer and arranged for the former bush pilot to fly Sky Dash for the interim. Then she called Addie.

"I'm staying with the Matteos for a few days," she said.

"Oh?" A world of questions revolved in that single word.

"Please call Kat and Mom for me. I don't have the energy right now." And she described her afternoon— from the minute she stepped into Rogan's office intending to explain her relationship to Abner Air, until the present.

"How are you feeling now?" Addie asked solicitously.

"Perfectly fine. The cramps are gone." All was back

to normal, although exhaustion—something the doctor had pointed out, as well—had her eyes drifting shut.

"I had them with all three of my pregnancies," Addie remarked.

"I don't recall you being forced into a vacation," Lee grumbled.

"Not a vacation, but I took a week last December because the doctor felt I was getting burned out with all the Christmas events on top of teaching and a gazillion other things."

"Except Skip still went to work." Her brother-in-law, a former NFL quarterback, taught and coached at Firewood High.

"Sure," Addie said, "but he came home at noon and during study periods. He also let the assistant coaches take the team for the week."

"Rogan wants to stay home with me," Lee murmured. She peered over her shoulder through the window. He stood in the kitchen concocting tonight's dinner that, he said, was a secret with nineteen herbs and spices. Lee smiled. Would he use some of the ones growing fresh on the windowsill, the plants she'd bought two weeks ago?

"The man cares for you, sis. It was obvious the day I got the leg cramp."

"He says he's *so in like* with me, and from the way he said it, oh, Addie, it sounded too close to…"

"In love?"

"In less than a month?" she wailed softly. "No one falls that fast."

"Sometimes, Lee, that's how it happens. Question is, how do *you* feel toward him?"

"I think about him a hundred times a day. Minimum."

"That all?" Addie chortled. "So what's the problem?"

"They're not all good thoughts."

"Okay, that's bad. What are the not-so-good thoughts?"

Again Lee explained her reservations. "I was going to tell him today and then…"

"You had a tiny medical crisis. Okay, here's my advice. Go tell him. Immediately. If he throws a fit, call and I'll come get you."

Lee shivered even though the afternoon sun had jacked the temperature into the seventies. They talked a few more minutes before saying goodbye. Minutes later, Rogan stepped through the front door with a pot of tea and tray of sandwiches. "This will hold you until dinner," he told her.

"You didn't have to do this. I could've come inside."

"But then you wouldn't be able to enjoy the day." He set the tray on a small round ceramic table, handed her a plate stacked with sandwiches. "Turkey, lettuce, tomatoes, cukes, mayo on multi-grain bread."

"Thank you." She took a half, but didn't eat. She wished she'd brought a heavier jacket and blamed her abrupt chill on the spring breeze sifting through the trees from the ocean. "Rogan, I need to tell you something. And you need to listen."

She watched him pour the tea. Peppermint, she'd told him once, settled her stomach. He'd remembered.

"If this is about what I said in the car earlier," he said, sitting back. "It doesn't matter if you don't feel the same. No, I'll be honest." His smile was faint. "I'd be heartbroken, but I'll live. I have before."

Meaning his wife and daughter.

Lee placed the heels of her hands against her forehead and shut her eyes. When she found her balance, when she could speak, she turned her head. "I used to fly for Abner Air. My plane—the one you flew in—used to be part of that fleet. I obtained it as a divorce settlement. Rogan," she said, watching his smile ebb, his mouth tighten. "My ex owns Abner Air. It's him you're suing."

He didn't respond, and it gave her courage. "I'd quit the company four months before your wife's—that plane went down. However, when I flew for Abner, regulations were strict. If they hadn't been, I would not have worked there, and that's a fact."

"Why didn't you tell me this before?" he asked quietly.

"Because I was afraid that maybe you'd…." *See me as part of the tragedy. The way you're looking at me now.* "That you would judge my past."

He looked toward the pasture. The horses stood swishing their tails in the sunshine. "If what you're saying is true, that things were different when you worked for your ex, then your past has nothing to do with my problem."

"If? That's sounds convincing." Lee pushed out of the rocking chair. "Maybe we should rethink my stay here."

She plucked her cell phone from the table set with the lunch tray. Addie could drive her back to Burnt Bend, back to her apartment where she should have gone in the first place instead of listening to a smooth-talking lawyer.

He sprang to his feet. "Give me a minute," he said, closing the phone in her hand.

"It's okay, Rogan. Really. I wouldn't want me around, either."

"Stop. I'm trying to apologize, Lee." His shoulders heaved on a breath. "Look, I'm a mess, I admit that. This issue with Abner Air has gnawed at my gut for three years, and sometimes I can't think straight. But I made you a promise at the clinic, and I'd like to follow through. Please stay. If not for me, for Danny."

Out of earshot, the boy pushed his toy vehicles around the roots of the old oak. Lee's chest ached. In the car, the little guy *had* been excited to see her, babbling about his day and the videogames they could play together tonight.

"All right," she said. "For Danny." With that she carried her uneaten sandwich into the house.

Chapter Ten

Rather than focusing on what Lee had told him about her relationship to Stuart Hershel and Abner Air, Rogan listened to her sweet feminine giggles along with his son's squeals of delight in the living room.

He'd made her a promise at the clinic. But it was more than that. His feelings for her were intensifying each day. *We all have our history,* he thought as he cleaned the dinner dishes, and heard Danny laugh again. This moment, all Rogan cared about was his son's happiness. He couldn't ignore the fact she was also the first woman since Darby he'd brought home. *The first to stay overnight.*

The concept had his groin hardening.

Get a grip, Matteo. The last thing on her mind is sex.

Yet, he'd caught her looks across the table during dinner. Looks which were shy and sweet and—worried.

He hated thinking he might have put that worry in her eyes. That his behavior on the porch might have given her second thoughts, or that his almost-admission in the car could jeopardize this…*voltage*…between them.

Another bubble of laughter from the living room reinstated his smile. Until he wondered if she'd giggled with her soldier. Probably.

Guilt flashed through him. God, he felt as though he'd betrayed something sacrosanct by falling for Lee.

And there stood the truth.

He *was* falling for her. He hadn't said the exact words in the car, but he'd wanted to. Oh, yeah, he had wanted to set them—three prized treasures—into her hands: *I love you.*

Finished with the dishes, he walked to the living room.

She lounged in a corner of the sofa, and for an instant all Rogan saw were her pale, bare feet—her sexy feet—peeking from the afghan. *Wow,* was all he could think. A more beautiful sight he had yet to see. She'd taken the crimpy blue thing from her hair, letting the mass spill as a crimson waterfall across her shoulders and down her back. The lamplight gilded her cheeks and shimmered along the tips of her eyelashes.

Danny sat on the floor with a green sofa pillow clutched against his chest and stared up at Lee, and for a second the word "devotion" flickered into Rogan's mind.

Own up, pal. You're not far from it yourself.

"Dad." Danny beamed when he caught sight of him.

Lee straightened to a sitting position. "I was telling him a story." Pink touched her skin.

Rogan joined them. "You were, huh?" He lifted an eyebrow. "Videogames already boring?"

"Yeah, but guess what, Dad?" Danny jumped to his feet. "Lee used to play in the loft with her friend, Eve. They had a swing rope and jumped in the hay and everything. Isn't that cool?"

They'd been discussing the barn? "Well," he said, trying for nonchalance, as if jumping in haylofts were an everyday thing. "The barn was probably in better shape when *Miss* Lee was little, Dan."

"Built the summer before I was ten," she granted. "And I told him to drop the Miss." She pushed a lock of hair from the boy's eyes. "I think we've passed that phase."

Something warm streaked through Rogan. Clearing his throat, he said, "Time for bed, buddy."

Danny kissed Lee's cheek. "'Night. And don't forget," he whispered.

"I won't. I'll make a list tonight."

A list? "Be right back," Rogan told her.

"Take your time."

Upstairs, he waited as Danny washed up, brushed his teeth and got into his pajamas. After the boy climbed into bed and Rogan read a few pages from *The Hobbit,* he turned off the lamp.

"I like Lee, Daddy," Danny whispered when Rogan kissed his hair, damp from the washcloth. "She tells cool stories. Think she'll tell me another again, real soon?"

Rogan's heart ached. "I hope so, buddy."

"She's gonna help me pick names for the farm."

Ah. The list. "That's great, son. I can't wait to see which one you'll choose. 'Night now."

"'Night." He snuggled down, then popped back up. "Can we get a puppy? Bobby's dog had a litter and he's giving all nine of 'em away." Danny's gaze was fixated on Rogan. "He says they'll be ready for homes in six weeks 'cause their eyes are finally open."

"Sure. We'll pick one out next weekend."

"Yay! Can Lee come, too?"

"If she has the time. Now, it's time for sleep." After plugging in the night-light and partially closing the door, Rogan went downstairs. The living room was empty, the afghan gone. He strode through the rooms to the front door.

"There you are," he said, stepping outside. She sat again in the wooden rocker. Although the night temperature was warmer than usual, he said, "Let me get you a coat before you catch a chill."

"The blanket is plenty warm."

He came to stand by her chair. "Sure?"

Looking up, she smiled. "I never knew a lawyer could worry so much. I thought they saw everything through analytical eyes."

Laughing quietly, he sat in the second chair. "Only on the job. The rest of the time we're as human as the next guy."

They gazed at the thumbnail moon climbing the sky.

"Did you get someone to take your route?"

"Peyton Sawyer. He lives on the island."

"I know Peyton." Last week, the Desert Storm vet had come in to Rogan's office to discuss his VA pension. He said, "Seems he was one helluva fighter pilot."

"He was," Lee agreed, and he sensed her eyes drilling him. When Rogan remained silent, she went on, "I'm grateful for his experience."

"But…?"

"Nothing. I'd rather be the one flying my plane."

"This won't be the last time you'll need his help, Lee." Once the pregnancy advanced, the doctors would give the no-fly order. Not something she would take lightly, he imagined.

"Don't remind me."

"Have you thought what you might do?"

As they contemplated the night, she remained silent. On the breeze drifted the intermittent sound of the ocean, while in the pasture the murky shapes of the horses moved closer to the fence. At one point, a low nicker floated through the dark and Rogan wondered if the foal wandered from Juniper's side.

Into the quiet, Lee said, "I'm going to sell Sky Dash."

The statement wasn't one he expected. "Selling is rather final. There have to be other options."

She pushed out of the chair. "I don't know any." With the blanket wrapped around her, she burrowed her hands into the wool. "Would you mind if I went to bed? It's been a long day."

Rogan wanted to hold her, to tell her everything would be okay, just as she had in the days he'd sat in her plane. Instead, he laid an arm around her shoulder and his lips against her hair. "Come. I'll show you your room."

He led her to a guest room next to his home office on the main floor. During the daylight hours, the windows faced the backyard fringed by a copse of birch. In some ways, it was his favorite room. Peaceful and solitary, it spoke to him. Under the window stood a bed, which he'd made up with sheets and covered with a blue-and-gold comforter before he had stepped onto the porch.

Waiting at the door, he observed her walk over and

sink down on the quilt. "Thank you, Rogan." Her eyes hung on his. "See you in the morning?"

"I'll be here, but sleep as late as you want, and if you need something in the night the fridge is stocked."

"All I need is sleep."

"Okay." He hesitated, wanting more than anything to step inside and kiss her mouth, her tired eyes, and hold her through the night. Just hold her. But she didn't encourage him, so he nodded once, patted the doorframe and left.

In her dream, Lee heard a floorboard creak.

Her eyes snapped open to a tarry blackness.

She hadn't heard the creak in her dream. She heard it somewhere on the main floor, possibly the living room, forty steps from where she lay under the downy quilt.

A light went on, its faint, yellow hue filling the lengthy two-inch rectangle of her semi-closed door. Since childhood, she slept with her door ajar, not closed. Closed meant she couldn't hear things that went bump in the night.

The way they were now....

The refrigerator door thumped shut; a glass filled. Rogan, she suspected. Pressing the night-glow button on her wristwatch—1:38—she waited for him to finish and head back up the stairs.

The light went out. For two heartbeats silence rang through the house, then she heard the floorboard creak again and his soft footfalls come down the hallway to her room. At her door, he paused and she wondered if he would enter…but no, he retraced his steps.

She pushed back the covers, hurried across the room.

"Rogan," she called quietly—before she had time to evaluate what she was about to do. At the hall entrance she could see his tall frame stop and turn.

"Lee?" He returned down the hall. "You're awake."

"What did you want?" She wished she could see his eyes in the night. Wished he wore more than a pair of sweat pants. At arm's length, his naked chest mainlined a male musk into her blood.

"I just wanted to make sure you were okay," he said. "That you weren't having any more cramps."

She took his hand, kissed his knuckles. "I'm aware things can go wrong. Stuart and I tried for years to get pregnant. Once I thought I was, then the next month I wasn't. The stress of trying ended our marriage." *Along with his betrayal.* "Thank you for being so concerned."

His touch caressed her neck, traveled to her cheek. "Do you know how much I want to take you to bed right now?"

Catching his wrist, she pressed his palm against her collarbones where her heart rate gathered speed. "Me, too."

"Lee…"

"It's okay, Rogan."

"This isn't a good idea. We can't—I mean… Hell, now you'll think all I want is sex when that's not what you need right now."

"Who says I don't need it?"

"But your cramps…"

"Come and gone. I haven't felt anything since noon. I'm okay, really." She offered a shy smile. "Will Danny be okay for an hour?"

"Yeah." A tweak of amusement tugged at his voice. "He's practically unconscious."

"All right, then." Taking his hand, she led him into the guest room, and to the narrow bed. Selfish or not, she wanted this night with him. She wanted a man's arms around her for a few hours. *Not a man's—Rogan's.* When had she begun feeling these deep emotions, deeper than what she'd felt for any man, including her husband?

The moment you met this man.

Mentally, she slapped the thought away. This was a night for creature comforts. What had her friend, Lily, said this afternoon when Lee called the doctor for a second opinion? *"You need down time. Go to a spa, have a pedicure, read a book. Heck, go out on a date…"*

A date with benefits, perhaps?

Except deep in her core, Lee's spirit rebelled. This was not a "with benefits" situation. This dealt with the heart.

Pressing her lips together, she climbed beneath the quilt. The moon's pale light washed the unadorned window, acclimatizing her eyes to the night, to him.

"Rogan?" Hoping her hands were steady, she held the comforter open in welcome.

Motionless, he stood by the bed, looking down at her. "Do you have any idea how sexy you are wearing my T-shirt with your hair down?" Leaning in, he gave her an openmouthed kiss. "And in the moonlight."

She flushed. "I like wearing your shirt. It brings you closer."

Slipping beside her, he snuggled her into his arms, kissed her again. "How's this for closeness?"

"Much better." She felt his rising strength press

against her stomach as they lay in the cozy confines of the bed.

In her mouth his tongue was a dueling partner. Under her shirt his palm and fingers tenderly touched her sensitized breasts.

"Ah, Lee. So warm, so soft." More kissing. "I want to make love with you more than anything in the world."

"I want to make love, too."

Through the loose flannel of his sweats, his arousal stood hard, ready. Closing her hand around him, she catalogued his size and shape through the soft fabric.

A groan rumbled from his chest and he tugged her fingers free. "Stop or I'll lose control."

"I want you to lose it," she whispered, slipping her hand into his sweats, diving for the heat, the steel of him.

"Lee." Again, he captured her hands. Fingertip kisses punctuating his words, he chided, "Give me a minute. It's been a long time and I'd rather not react like a randy teenager with you. I want to go slow, be a gentleman."

Smiling against his chest, she inhaled his scent. "All that Southern hospitality makes me so hot." He intoxicated her with his sensitivity, his concern. "I won't break, Rogan. I promise."

"I couldn't handle it if something went wrong… afterwards."

He was thinking of Darby. Lee stroked his chest, his flat abdomen. She did not want his dead wife in their bed. She did not want Abner Air in this bed. Or Stuart or Oliver. Tonight was hers and Rogan's. "Let's get naked," she said, catching hold of his waistband.

"You sure?"

"Oh, yeah."

For a fistful of seconds, they lay still, then both reacted at once, stripping shirts and sweats and panties until they were flesh to flesh and he had his tongue in her mouth, and she wriggled her body under his weight. Her legs secured his hips and she towed him into her before he had time to change his mind.

"Lee," he cried, a joyful sound that sent a sweet current streaming through her veins.

She drove her hands into the thickness of his hair, over his shoulders, down the curve of his spine, discerning the plane of his body with her palms, while his mobile kisses vacillated from passionate to tender and back again, and she thought she might faint from the pleasure. Hips bumping hers, he began to move.

Slowly, sensually.

"Lee," he said again. "You've caught my heart."

She replied with long, lingering kisses.

After a few moments, he rolled with her so she rested above him. "This is easier for you," he whispered.

His consideration stung her eyes.

"You okay?"

"Don't stop. I'm flying."

His chest vibrated on a chuckle. "My sweet pilot. I'll fly with you forever." He stroked her hair, her breasts; rested his large, warm hands against the microscopic mound of her stomach. Moonlight dipped through the window, touched his serious mouth.

"Come here," he said, bringing her down on his chest.

With utmost care, he moved against her—curve to angle, soft to hard, texture to taste. And when at last they flew into the night, she hung his name in the stars.

* * *

Resting her head on his chest, she listened to the strong tempo of his heart as he toyed with her fingers on his belly.

"I love you, Lee," he said in a deep, quiet voice. "I want to marry you, give the baby a family."

"Oh, my," she whispered, panic and wonder tripping her pulse rate. "The moon really does affect the psyche."

"It's not the moon," he said gruffly. "Just the truth."

She couldn't speak, couldn't breathe. "I thought…"

"That I was simply keeping a vow I made at the clinic? That I'd walk away once you healed?"

"This afternoon you wanted me to stay for Danny's sake."

"This afternoon I didn't know how else to keep you here, how else to convince you to stay for *our* sake."

Her heart banged her ribs. He loved her. He wanted to marry her. He wanted her to live in this lovely, old house as a family. He was proposing—in a roundabout way—what she knew her father offered Charmaine thirty-seven years ago, after they conceived Lee.

And you know how that ended.

Three years later, Steven Tait walked away from his wife and daughter, never to return.

Lee chewed the inside of her cheek. Rogan was not Steven Tait. He already had a child and he had not made Lee pregnant.

But the scenario embraced too many similarities— and adversities. And she had yet to talk about Abner Air, expand on what she'd told him tonight on his porch.

But, oh…could she take a chance on him? *Should* she?

"We've known each other what, three weeks?" she

asked, pursuing the logical element of the argument. "Only teenagers fall in love that quick."

"I never fell in love until I was twenty-two and met Darby."

"Was it fast with her, too?"

"No, we were friends first. She was studying to be a paralegal. We'd meet in this coffee house to talk textbook cases. As time went on things got more serious and about two years from the day we met, we married. And even then I wasn't aware she had depression problems. She didn't tell me until five months after the wedding."

"Are you saying you wouldn't have married her if you'd known?"

"Not at all. I loved her. But had she trusted me from the get-go, our marriage might have been stronger. I might have been able to prepare better for our future. And I wouldn't have felt…I don't know…like I wasn't trustworthy."

"Maybe she was afraid to tell you," Lee whispered, thinking of her own secret, of the pilot flying Darby into a forest, the pilot Lee should have reported.

"Maybe," he conceded.

"And sometimes a person isn't as strong as they would like to be, or as others perceive them to be. Sometimes there are invisible factors beneath the surface they'd rather keep hidden."

Rogan shifted so his head lay on her pillow, his face inches from hers. "What is it, Lee? What are you trying to say? That you're not a good person because you own a plane that once belonged to the man responsible for taking shortcuts with his fleet?"

Her pulse pounded behind her tongue. "The plane has nothing to do with it."

"Then what?"

"Nothing. Let's go to sleep." As if she could.

He touched her lips with his thumb. "I'll be forty soon. I've seen a lot in the seventeen years since I met Darby and, yes, it's been less than a month since you and I met. But I know what I want in life, what I feel. Right here." He tapped his chest. "That said, if you need time, honey, take it." He kissed her nose. "I'm not going anywhere."

"And if I still say no?"

He kissed her eyes, tarried at her lips. "I hope you won't. But if you do, then it'll be a lesson in patience."

"Until I say yes?"

"Until your heart says yes."

"You could be a very old man by then."

"Maybe."

"You don't sound worried."

"On the contrary, I'm crazy with worry. You're an intelligent, independent woman, and it scares the hell out of me."

She had no comeback. So she lay clasped in his arms, trying to sort through what his statement conjured: that he saw her as entirely different from his wife.

Except I'm not, Lee thought. *I have secrets, too.*

Chapter Eleven

Danny complained about a stomachache the next morning, prompting Rogan to leave a message with the school that his son would not be in class today. Yet when Lee observed the child dig into a bowl of Cheerios minutes later, she wondered if Danny wasn't averse to playing a little hooky.

The moment Rogan hung up the phone, the child sent her a shy, juice-painted smile across the table and she knew her intuition was right. The boy wasn't sick; he wanted to stay with her.

The notion enveloped her warm as a blanket. It appeared Danny liked her a lot.

But it wasn't reason enough for him to stay home from school. She was about to pull Rogan aside and explain her suspicions when her cell phone beeped on the counter, indicating a voicemail. Checking the number, she frowned. *Stuart?* What did *he* want? They hadn't spoken in years, not since they stood in a courtroom and a judge decreed Stuart concur to Lee's decisions.

"Something wrong?" Rogan asked, pouring another cup of coffee.

"I don't know, but I have to take this."

"Need my office for some privacy?"

"That's fine. I'll go out on the porch." She tossed him a smile to conceal her worry. "I love early mornings. Be back in a minute."

Grabbing his wool-lined jacket from the mudroom, she took her cup of peppermint tea outside. To the west, a storm system approached. She would need to call Peyton Sawyer as soon as she called her ex-husband. She clicked Reply.

"Stuart Hershel."

"It's Lee Tait," she said, wanting to drive home the point she no longer carried his name. "How did you get my number?"

"What difference does it make?"

"The difference is, Stuart, you are not to contact me. Ever. That's what lawyers are for."

"Point taken. As we speak my lawyer is calling yours. We're going back to court. I want the divorce settlement reassessed."

"Why?"

"Because I want my seaplane back."

She snorted. "Excuse me, but that plane was my reason for not taking you to the cleaners. You got the house and the business. I got one damned plane and a scant twenty thousand dollars."

"My best plane, my only *sea*plane. I want it back."

"What's this about? Your wife needing a new mansion?"

Through the gossip mill Lee heard he'd moved from the suburbs, from the Tudor-style house she had once made home, to a three-acre property with an ocean view.

"Don't be snide. It doesn't suit you."

"Yeah, well. I learn fast. Especially after seeing my husband boffing a barmaid under *my* quilt." Actually the quilt had been on the floor, which left far more to the eye than Lee ever wanted to experience again.

"My wife," he ground out, "was not a barmaid."

"Pardon my mistake. Waitress, I meant waitress."

He was silent. The wind cut into her jacket and brought drops of rain to dot the porch railing. He said, "She still has more class than you."

"What she has is more ass than me."

Across the miles, Lee heard his breathing accelerate. "I'm getting my plane back, Lee, and that's a promise."

"Right, and here's *my* promise. If you bring this back to court I'll come after your house, and don't think I won't get it. You knew about Bill Norton's drinking problem."

"What drinking problem?"

She barked a laugh. "The one that had him smelling like a vat of sour beer the day you hired him." Upon finding Stuart in bed with the waitress, Lee had quit him and his company on the spot. However, when he signed on Bill Norton to take her place, she had voiced her reservations, and the rumors rotating the flight circuit.

He should be reported to the FAA, she'd told Stuart.

You're the one leaving on short notice, he'd snapped, *and I need a pilot.*

Short notice. When she added the months to the child's birth, he'd bedded the waitress two months before Lee caught him. Short notice, indeed.

"Norton was an experienced pilot." Stuart snuffed her memories. "Sure he tied one on every now and again, but he never flew drunk. He was always sober when he got behind the controls. You can talk about this until the cows come home, Lee, but he was not drunk on that flight."

She heard his voice tremble. "Believe what you want."

"You bet I will. He was my wife's cousin. I knew him."

"Your wife's...*cousin?*" Dear God, could it get any worse?

"I'm getting that plane back whether you like it or not. Besides," he said, his tone hard again. "You got an excellent rep. Any company would hire you. I'll put in a voucher."

She didn't want to work for any company. Nor did she need his commendation. Sky Dash was hers and until *she* figured out how to run it plus raise a child or, heaven help her, sell the business, no one—least of all Stuart Hershel—had the right to map her future.

"I'll cut you a deal," he ranted, reeling Lee back to the conversation at hand. "A trade straight across the board."

"Trade?"

"The seaplane for the ten acres at Moses Lake. You sell those, you buy any seaplane your little heart desires," Stuart said, and Lee pictured him puffing out his chest over the offer. "Either way, we're both in the money."

At that she laughed. "You haven't been able to sell that swamp in six years."

"The right buyer hasn't come along, is all. Look." His voice took an edge. "You got the time to wait. I don't."

Ah, she thought. *Of course.* He needed her plane for no other reason than to sell it so he could pay the compensation Rogan no doubt demanded in his lawsuit.

Hugging his coat around her, she stared through the misty rain at the foal huddled against its mother's side. Last night Rogan had held her to his body, kissed and touched her and talked about marriage. And now Stuart wanted her seaplane because Norton's inebriation had been a death warrant.

Why, *why* hadn't she reported the man to the FAA? *Because after the bed scene your mind went AWOL.*

"I'll fight you tooth and nail," she said, more angry than she'd been in three years. *Ass.* Shutting off the phone so he couldn't call back, she wheeled around—and jerked to a stop.

Danny stood ten feet away. "What's a vat of sour beer?"

"Should you be outside, honey?" And where was Rogan that he hadn't caught his son heading out the door in his pj's with no coat or footwear?

"I'm not cold," Danny replied, breath foggy as he spoke.

Trying not to focus on how long he might have listened to her one-sided conversation—or what he understood—Lee ushered him into the warmth of the mudroom. "You're sick," she chided gently. "Sick boys stay in bed and don't go outside."

"Well…" came the sheepish reply, "I kinda feel okay now."

"Do you now? Have you told Dad?"

"No, but I wanna stay an' keep you company. Dad said you were sick and I don't want you to be sick."

Ho-boy. "Danny." Lee pushed the hair from his somber eyes. "I'm honored you want to stay with me, but it's not right to make up stories, especially to your dad. Besides, I'm not really sick." *Oh, heck.* He'd know soon enough anyway. "I'm going to have a baby so the doctor wants me to take it easy for a couple of days."

His brown eyes widened. "Really?"

"Yep. But let's keep it our secret for now, all right?"

"Doesn't Dad know?"

"Yes, and now you do, too. So, it's just the three of us. Okay?"

Nodding eagerly, he zippered a finger across closed lips, then tossed the invisible key over his shoulder.

"That's my boy," she said and hugged him. "Now go tell Dad you're going to school."

Danny dashed for the stairwell that led to his bedroom. "Dad," he shouted. "Hurry! I gotta go to school."

Rogan poked his head out of the office across from the guest room where she'd lain with him last night. "What's going on?"

"Danny has something to tell you." Lee sank onto the living room couch, suddenly tired. A conversation with Stuart felt like a two-day marathon.

Rogan walked over to kiss her hair, a touch she was beginning to crave far too much. "You all right?"

"I'm fine." She caught his hand. "Go easy on him, Rogan. He was just worried about me."

"I know." And for a split second she saw something in his expression that made her think of the missing piece haunting his life for three years. Family.

Her heart hurt as she thought of the conversation they would have later, the secret she still needed to share.

"See you in a bit," he whispered. Less than ten minutes later, she heard the mudroom door close, then his truck start.

On the sofa and under the knitted blanket, she listened to the rain pummel the house—and she waited. Waited for him to return so she could eradicate that hunger, *that wish,* from his heart with six words....

The plane crashed because of me.

Driving through the storm, Rogan knew something was amiss.

For twenty minutes he'd sat behind the wheel, en route to Burnt Bend Elementary, listening to Danny's chatter, then reversing the direction, and he hadn't been able to shake off the presage of doom.

Last night had been terrific. He'd held Lee in his arms until dawn spilled through the windows. Throughout the night, between bouts of sleep, they had kissed and talked, and kissed some more. He should feel exhausted; instead he felt exhilarated.

He loved her.

He never believed it could happen, his loving another woman. With Darby he'd been a protector, her defender against life's inconsistencies, its drama.

Lee, on the other hand, exuded an inner strength that attracted him as nothing had before. Yet, at the heart of all her independence lay a vulnerability he wanted to safeguard.

She sat on the padded rocker on the front porch. The wind danced with her thick ponytail, and blew strands across her cheeks. Through the windshield, hazy with raindrops the moment he shut off the engine and wipers, he took in her woolen green jacket, brown slacks and tall black boots. The overnight bag next to her feet.

Feigning calmness, he climbed the porch stairs. "Going somewhere?" he asked.

"I've called my mother to drive me home. But before she gets here, I need to explain something."

He parked his butt against the railing, crossed his arms to ward off a rising chill from within. "Sounds ominous."

She glanced away. The ponytail accented the hollowness of her cheeks. In her lap, she held her house keys in a death grip. Slowly, her gaze wove back, and the despair he saw constricted his windpipe.

"The call I got before you left was from my ex-husband."

Rogan remained stone still. Raindrops tapped his shoulders, crept under his collar.

"Stuart wants to revisit the divorce settlement."

"What settlement? All you got was a plane."

"His best plane."

"And now he wants to reclaim it?"

"Yes." Again she looked toward the pasture, and the horses with their tails to the rain. "He's willing to trade."

"Trade. Let me guess, the trade is in his favor. You get junk in return." Rogan deduced the reason behind the whole distasteful scenario and it sent a feral craving through him. He yearned to lash out. Preferably at Stuart Hershel.

"Not junk. Ten acres of wilderness."

"Where?"

"About forty minutes from Moses Lake."

Rogan stared at her. "That's in the middle of nowhere. You didn't agree. Please, say you didn't, Lee."

"I said I'd fight him."

"Good girl."

"But I probably won't because there's something else."

And then she told him about her husband's infidelity.

"I found them in our bed, braided together like ropes. I couldn't believe how calm I was, standing in the doorway. All I said was, 'I'm outta here,' and went to the flight service office. About ten minutes later Stuart came in. I'd emptied my desk already and had started on the file cabinets. Do you know what he said? 'Please stay, Lee. Stay until I find another pilot.'" Her laugh was brittle. "Not stay in the marriage, but until he got another pilot to take my place."

"Bastard," Rogan murmured. If the man ever showed his face…

"So I stayed one week. Because I couldn't let my passengers down. Bill Norton showed up on my last morning smelling worse than a brewery. I told Stuart I suspected the man was an alcoholic. He said he had checked his references, that he was clean."

Her face crumpled momentarily; she lifted her chin. "Stuart was extremely finicky about his pilots. He wanted the best. So I believed he'd done his homework. His betrayal in our marriage should've been a signal." Her eyes pierced Rogan. "Forty minutes ago I found out Norton was a cousin to Stuart's mistress."

Against his body, Rogan's fingers fisted. He wanted to strangle Stuart Hershel slowly. The man had ruined the lives and memories of two families.

Lee went on, "It wasn't until I heard about the crash four months later that I realized Stuart hadn't followed my advice. That's why I'm to blame," she whispered, swiping a tear off her cheek. "It's my fault. *I* should've reported Norton."

Rogan scarcely breathed. Finally he knew. Finally the puzzle behind his family's demise fell into place. He recalled Sophie's happy smile, her parting words as he walked them to the taxi waiting at the curb of their house to take them to the airport, *Love you, Daddy.*

He wanted to crush rocks with his bare hands, release the festering rage he'd harbored for thirty-eight months.

To kill the man responsible.

"Why," he asked, forcing an enormous calm into his voice, "didn't you explain this before?"

"I wanted to. I really did. But I didn't know how or where to begin. And there was this…attraction between us and I…I thought you might see me as a bad person. Which is wrong and selfish of me, I know." She drew in a long breath.

Rogan uncrossed his arms, gripped the railing behind. Rain beat the earth behind him, gushed from the eaves troughs. "If that's what you think, Lee, then you don't know me very well."

Taking up her overnight bag, she rose. "I agree. I don't. Nor do I know what your intentions are for the future. Or whether you'll still feel—"

"The same way about you?" He stepped into her

space. "That it? You're worried whether I'll still want to marry you?"

"Yes," she said and he saw her top lip quiver.

"Why?"

"Because…"

"Why, Lee?"

Distress in her eyes, she glanced away.

Finger under her chin, he tugged her back gently. *"Why?"*

"Because," she cried. "I love you. There. Are you satisfied? But there won't be an end to this tragedy between us, Rogan. Bill Norton should've had his wings clipped. But the worst of it is I expected my husband to do the right thing and report him." She let out a caustic laugh. "A man who cheated." Eyes swimming, she pushed past him as the sound of a vehicle approached. "My mother's here. I have to go."

Before he could say another word or call her back, she was down the steps. A second later, she hauled open the pickup's door. He glimpsed an older version of Lee at the wheel. Then the truck U-turned to vanish down the lane among the trees, and he was left standing under a wet, gothic canopy of sky.

"Why are you crying?" Charmaine Wilson asked, turning onto the main route back to town.

Lee faced the side window. "I'm not crying."

"I can see that. Your eyes are red and puffy, you're sniffing and you sprinted down those steps as if your life depended on it. What'd he do to you?"

"He didn't do anything, Mom, and I don't want to talk about it. It's…" *Over.* "Never mind."

"Fine. Be that way."

"Look," Lee said wearily. "Can we not do this right now?"

Across the cab, Charmaine sighed. "Oh, Lee."

"Mom. Leave it, okay?"

They rode in silence for two minutes before Charmaine said, "I'm worried about you. You don't call for weeks, you barely visit anymore. And then out of the blue you tell me you're pregnant with Oliver Duvall's child, and now I'm picking you up from some strange man's house—"

"He's not a stranger. He's a friend." *Was a friend.* In truth he'd been so much more. He was the man she loved. *Loved.* The fervent, turn-your-insides-to-mush, forever-and-ever kind she'd never experienced.

Ten years older than Lee, Stuart had taught her how to fly before hiring her into his company. Shortly thereafter, they'd married. Admittedly, love had been part of it—until it was determined her body wasn't a fan of his sperm and he went elsewhere for a baby she'd wanted more than he had.

And there was Oliver…dear Oliver, her childhood best friend, a man with whom she created a baby, and whom she might have married *simply because.*

But Rogan…Rogan had held her heart in his palm the moment they met beside her aircraft, and he'd wrapped that soft Southern accent around her name.

"He's a friend," she repeated.

Charmaine kept her gaze on the road. "Sure he is."

"What's that supposed to mean?"

"It means that when you stay at a man's house overnight, he's not just a friend, Lee."

"And you would know," she snapped, and cringed. No matter the past, her mother didn't deserve to be treated without respect. "Sorry. I shouldn't have said that."

"But why wouldn't you think it?" Approaching town, her mother flicked the signal left for the street that led down to the boardwalk and Lee's apartment. "At times propriety wasn't on my horizon," Charmaine admitted. "I mean, three men, three daughters? I know what people thought, what they whispered."

Lee studied her mother. "It wasn't all bad," she said, realizing that too was a truth.

Yes, there had been mistakes. Omitting the logistics for Steven Tait leaving his three-year-old toddler was the first; hiding the name of Kat's father was another; forcing Addie to give up her baby fourteen years ago was the third blunder.

But in all, Lee and her sisters had had a good childhood. More often than not, laughter echoed through the blue-and-white house on the outskirts of town. Sure, there were sibling rivalries, and her mother still had a knack for meddling in the concerns of her daughters three decades later, albeit the meddling had ebbed over the last ten years. But upon reflection, Lee was mildly surprised to realize she wouldn't change her childhood.

Charmaine pulled into the parking lot behind Coffee Sense and cut the engine. Gripping the steering wheel, she continued, "I know you all think I'm a bad mother."

"No, Mom. We don't."

"I really tried to raise you girls as best I could," Charmaine went on, staring at the wrought-iron stairway to Lee's apartment.

"And we all turned out fine." Her mother had never been prone to warm fuzzies, but Lee rubbed her shoulder anyway. "Let's go in and I'll make some tea."

Charmaine's eyes blurred. "Okay," she whispered. "I'd like that."

Inside, Lee put on the kettle while her mother walked to the curio to survey the heritage teapots. "You got a new one," she said, pointing to the Meissen with its shamrock-contoured handle.

"In January," Lee replied. Had it been four months since she invited her mother over? Shame flashed. Charmaine was not getting younger, and soon Lee would have a child. Right there and then, she vowed to do right, to make changes with her mother.

Walking over to stand beside the older woman, she slid an arm around Charmaine's waist. When had her mother gotten shorter? "You've never asked why I collect them," she said.

"I know why, honey. You always loved the one your daddy gave me on our wedding day. He loved them, so you do, too."

Surprised, Lee looked at her mother. Lines of life and laughter spooled from the corners of her eyes.

Charmaine smiled and surprised Lee further by setting a hand against her cheek. "You were always such a strong child, and so darn independent. Sometimes, you scared me because you seemed to fear nothing and no one."

Rogan said the same thing last night, she thought,

and realized she'd spoken aloud when Charmaine smiled. "Tell me about this Rogan," she said. "He's obviously important to you."

Lee's shoulders sagged. "Oh, Mom."

"Come." Charmaine took her hand, led her to the sofa. "Sit while I get the tea, then we'll talk."

Twenty minutes later and resting her head on the back of the couch, Lee said, "Now you know it all." Oliver, Rogan, the crisis in her pregnancy, Stuart's subterfuge. Her plans concerning Sky Dash.

Charmaine sat silent for a long minute. Finally she said, "I've never known you to give up so easily, Lee. You know this is a type of blackmail, what Stuart's demanding?"

Lee sighed. "Whether it is or not, I can't afford the court costs to fight him."

"I have a nice little nest egg. It's yours."

So strong was the swell of relief it stung Lee's eyes. "You'd do that?"

"Of course," Charmaine retorted. "You're my child, and that," she gestured to Lee's tummy, "is my grandchild. Did you really think I'd let that scum hurt you again?"

Lee reached out to grip her mother's hand. When had she last told her mother she loved her? *So long ago I can't remember.* "I love you, Mom," she said, nose prickling.

Charmaine's eyes lit. "I love you, too, baby. Now I'll bet your Rogan has a really good lawyer friend who can cinch this up nice and tight for you."

Lee slumped back. "He's not my Rogan. Besides, he doesn't want to see me again."

"Is that what he said?"

"Not in so many words." *You don't know me very well,* he'd said and she'd agreed. What more was there to say?

Charmaine refilled their cups. "Hmm. From what you've told me, he's not a man who takes things lightly."

"Precisely."

"Including asking a woman to marry him." Charmaine's eyebrows lifted. "Am I right?"

"Even if you were, Mom, I'll always know it was *my* fault for not reporting Bill Norton."

"Except it was Stuart's responsibility. It was his company. Have you forgotten how he made you sign a pre-nup before your wedding? One that excluded your rights to any part of the company?"

"Doesn't matter. *I* should've reported Norton." Lee covered her face.

"*You did.*" Charmaine grabbed Lee's wrists and tugged them down. Her eyes blazed blue fury. "You told the boss of the company. It was up to him to report the man. But he didn't, which was *his* choice. This isn't your fault, understand? *Not your fault.*"

Never before had Lee seen her mother so angry. For a moment she sat spellbound.

Charmaine went on: "For years I beat myself up over your daddy's leaving. Maybe I should've cooked better meals. Maybe I should've been sexier in the bedroom. Maybe I shouldn't have nagged him to get a better job. Maybe I should've loved him more. Bottom line, Lee? *He* chose to sever himself from us. *He chose that option.* Not me, not you. Only Steven Tait."

Lee sat stunned. Charmaine climbed to her feet, paced in front of the couch. "I promised myself I would never tell you this, but you're a grown woman, with a baby on the way and a man who loves you, waiting on that farm. Lee, your father had another family."

"What?"

"He had a year-old son with another woman. They lived down in Portland. He told me he couldn't live the lie anymore, couldn't support two families."

Mouth ajar, Lee gaped at her mother.

Charmaine shrugged. "He loved her."

"And not us?"

"Not *me*. He loved you."

"Well," Lee said, anger taking root. "He had a peculiar way of showing it."

Charmaine gazed at Lee before her mouth curved. "That savings account I mentioned? He opened it with five thousand dollars after you were born. Said to let it collect interest for a rainy day. I'd say that day has come, wouldn't you?"

Chapter Twelve

After Lee left, Rogan couldn't stay in the house, so he drove into town and sat at his office desk reviewing two cases he'd taken the previous Friday. One dealt with a property variance, the second was a messy divorce and custody case.

Amazing, he thought, how fast people require a lawyer when one's available.

He lifted his head and stared at the door. Lee could use a good lawyer. If it weren't for the conflict of interest…

For a long minute, he ruminated. Had her mother returned her to the apartment, or driven Lee to her childhood home?

He wanted to knock on the door across the landing. He wanted to see Lee. Most of all, he wanted to wrap her in his arms, say everything would be okay, that he had the answers to keep her plane, and would battle dragons to save Sky Dash.

He stayed seated and worked. He made and received calls, accepted three new cases, researched a point of law for Johnny, and put together an affidavit for a previous case from Renton.

And he thought of Lee. Of the night they spent together, cuddled into each other, alert to nuances… heartbeats, breathing, heat. He remembered how she looked coming out of the guest room, tousled and sleepy-eyed, snug in his navy blue terry robe. How her long, freckled fingers dipped the teabag into the hot water she'd boiled. Watching her, with the memory of her delicate china swirling in his brain, Rogan had wondered if tea tasted differently in large, thick mugs like those in his kitchen cupboards.

During lunch, he changed into his running gear and, for an hour, took to the spongy, tree-shadowed trail Lee and her sisters walked the day Addie's leg cramped.

And still he could not get her out of his head.

You might see me as a bad person, she had said, when all he saw was a woman of integrity.

At three o'clock, he drove to Danny's school.

"Is Lee home?" the boy asked, scrambling into the backseat.

"No, son. She went home with her mom."

"Aw. How come? Doesn't she like us no more?"

I love you. There. Are you satisfied?

Rogan caught his son's somber gaze in the rearview mirror. "She likes us." *More than.*

"Is she coming back?"

"I hope so."

"Can we go see her?"

"Not today." Not until they sorted out the problems she believed stood between them.

Danny rode in silence as Rogan turned onto Shore Road. He wondered what mulled through his son's head while the boy viewed the environment out the side window.

He didn't have long to wait.

"It's probably good Lee's staying with her mom." The rearview mirror reflected round brown eyes. "If I was sick I'd want you to stay home with me." Pause. "That's sorta like staying with a mom, right?"

Rogan swallowed. Memories of Darby could still pop up in unexpected ways. Sometimes, he welcomed them; sometimes, he wished them gone.

Today, he did not want to remember Darby. Not while his mind was full of Lee, and his chest aching with an emotion he was at a loss to clarify. Pure and simple, he wanted her back.

"Is it, Dad?" Danny repeated.

Ah, hell. How to explain the fine line of discrepancy? "Staying with either parent is good, son, because in most cases—in yours and Lee's—both parents love and care for their children very much. Dads, though, might play videogames with their kid, maybe give him a kiss or two on the head—" his style "—whereas moms might read to him and do lots of cuddling."

Again, Danny fell silent. "No offense, Dad," he said in a voice Rogan didn't recognize. "But when I'm sick, do you think we can ask Lee to stay over? I mean she bought me the digger, and she saved me from the loft, and tells stories and she smells really nice. Anyway," he added, staring out the window. "I really, really like her. Don't you?"

"Yeah, I do, Dan." *I'm crazy about her.*

"Good. 'Cause I think she'd be a great mom. What do you think?"

Lee floated in a deep dream. She knew it was a dream because one moment she drifted above the courtroom, and in the next she faced the female judge, whose long black robe dwarfed her petite frame.

Either way, Lee knew Judge Judy was far from weak. Her hazel eyes glimmered behind wire-rim glasses as she surveyed the defense table where Stuart sat with a smirk across his lips.

Beside Lee, her attorney rose and spoke. "Your Honor, I would like to begin by—"

Stuart's lawyer pushed to his feet, and it shocked Lee to see Bill Norton representing her ex. When had the pilot changed careers? she wondered, floating above the room again.

"Excuse me, Judge," Norton said, "but that woman—" he pointed at Lee "—is a gold digger. Not only has she cheated on my client, Mr. Hershel, by having another man's baby, but she's taken Mr. Hershel's most valuable plane without his permission. He's now bankrupt. Oh, and the latest news is she's shacked up with Rogan Matteo. God only knows what she's planning to take from him!"

"Mr. Norton!" The judge whacked her gavel on her mahogany desk; behind her the flag shuddered. "You are out of line. Sit down before I throw you to the wolves."

"No, Judge, the wolves say she's at fault. I did not fly

that plane drunk. She's making up stories the way she made them up for Danny about her wonderful childhood."

"Order, Mr. Norton." *Whack-whack!*

"I am in order, Judge. Did you know her daddy left her? Did you know Stuart and Oliver and Rogan left her?

"Mr. Norton!"

"Even her baby left. *Everyone leaves-leaves-leaves-leaves!*"

Lee wrenched awake. Her heart flailed her ribs. Her lungs screamed for air. Inside her mouth flowed the iron taste of blood. Gingerly, she touched her tongue to the lip her teeth clamped.

A nightmare, she'd had a nightmare. Norton wasn't alive. She wasn't in a courtroom. No judge sat on the bench. Her baby…

She touched her abdomen. *My baby's okay.*

Slowly, she waited for her pulse to calm, her vision to focus. Checking her wristwatch, she saw it was after midnight—and she lay in her childhood bed. After their talk over tea in the apartment, Charmaine had convinced Lee to stay with her in the little blue house where she'd grown from baby to woman.

Staring through the darkness, she contemplated the nightmare. For years she believed vivid dreams, the ones you remembered in detail, could tell you something if you read them close enough.

This one reeled in Technicolor with faces sharp and menacing.

Had the courtroom scene foretold a future, or an abridgment of her life?

Whatever, the dream illuminated one factor: nothing, *absolutely nothing,* mattered beyond her baby.

Stuart and his schemes could go to hell.

Rogan and his proposal… She would think of Rogan later, when her heart no longer ached this hard.

Right now, however, she needed to concentrate solely on making a home for her child. If that meant selling Sky Dash to the highest bidder in order to keep her business—*her assets*—out of the clutches of her ex-husband, so be it.

Thursday night, Rogan finished up the dinner dishes and called Johnny while Danny watched a sitcom.

"Hey, R.B.," his younger brother said. "I was just about to call you. Got some good news."

Rogan could imagine. Wasting no preliminaries, he said, "I need you to dump the lawsuit."

Silence. Then, "You're kidding, right?"

Rogan swiveled his desk chair around and gazed at the pink and orange aura the setting sun hung on the trees. "I'm dead serious."

"Mind explaining?"

"Long story short, it's been dragging me down for too long. I'm sick of it. I want to move on."

"Well," Johnny said. "That's noble and all, but we're this close—" Rogan imagined his brother creating an inch of space between thumb and index finger "—from getting a significant compensation. That's why I was about to call. Hershel's willing to meet our latest request."

"As of when?"

"This morning. I was in court all day and didn't get the news until I got back to the office a couple hours ago."

Rogan's hand clenched the phone. Of course Hershel

would roll over and submit; Lee probably agreed to the jerk's demands. Biting back a curse at the thought, Rogan said, "Fine, tell Hershel we'll take his original offer. The one from two years ago."

"Are you nuts? Now is not the time to start waffling—"

"It has nothing to do with waffling. The whole thing's been a ball and chain." He sighed. "I can't do it anymore, Johnny. It's twisted me inside and out and I just want to put an end to that part of my life. Danny's finding friends here, he's smiling and excited to go to school, and I'm enjoying my profession for the first time in years."

Again, silence hummed through the line. "You've found a woman."

"Yeah," Rogan admitted. "But that's another story."

"I got all night."

Rogan exhaled slowly. "All right," he said. "Don't interrupt until I'm finished." And then he told his brother about Lee, how he met her, why she walked away last Monday—and everything in between. When he was done, the only sound he heard was the wind gusting past the corners of the house.

Quietly, Johnny said, "Lee Tait is the source I told you about, the one I was attempting to track down for an interview."

Rogan swallowed. "Well, now you can forget about trying to contact her."

Another beat of silence. "So. Correct me if I'm wrong. You think she's decided to trade her seaplane, so the bastard can sell it to pay the amount we're currently demanding."

"Pretty much."

"Except you're *assuming* this is her real intention."

"I know Lee." Simply saying her name sent an ache through Rogan's bones.

"Huh. It's barely been a month since you met her, Ro. And she's going to help a man in conflict with her ex-husband?"

"I know Lee," he repeated stubbornly. He couldn't explain it. He simply felt her suffering with every cell in his body. The blame she harbored for that plane crash matched his own.

"All right," Johnny said finally. "If the original offer is what you want, consider it done. Later, though, I'll be putting out the word about Abner Air. They should face some music over this."

Rubbing a hand down his whiskered cheeks, Rogan drew a long breath. "Thanks, Johnny. I owe you."

"You don't owe me a damned thing. But I want to meet this Lee Tait. I want to meet the woman who's changed your perspective on life."

Rogan felt his lips curve. "If she'll have me."

"Why wouldn't she have you? After all," Johnny teased, "you are my brother." On a more serious note he added, "You're a good guy, R.B. You always were."

"So are you, li'l brother."

Johnny issued a soft chuckle. "I'm the family black sheep, or did you forget?"

"I form my own opinions," Rogan said.

"Good. I look forward to meeting your Lee."

His Lee. *Let's hope she'll be mine,* Rogan thought as he ended the call.

Through the open door across the hallway, he caught

sight of the bed he and Lee had slept in on Monday night. The night she'd curled into him as if she were seeking shelter.

Oh, yeah, hope was all he had.

Hope shrouded in fear that he might be too late.

Friday morning Lee stood in the entranceway of her childhood home. The last few days with her mother made her realize how much she loved this old, drafty house with its cabbage rose welcome mat and its wooden bar of coat hooks on the wall. However, it was time to leave, time to return to her apartment and her life.

An hour ago, she'd been to the Burnt Bend Medical Clinic. Both she and the baby were healthy and stable, and as long as Lee didn't lift objects over five pounds the pregnancy should stay on course. The doctor had given her permission to fly until her third trimester, at which time she would need to stay grounded and find some alternatives concerning Sky Dash.

The doctor's warning hadn't dampened her hopes. Already, the alternatives were in motion. Throughout the past three days, while convalescing on her mother's couch, Lee had been busy making phone calls. By the first of June—in four weeks—Sky Dash would belong to a Bremerton buyer, and she'd hang up her wings.

"I can't believe you're going through with this sale," Charmaine said, watching Lee shrug into her coat. "Flying has been your dream since you were ten years old."

"Dreams are for fairy tales. Being married to Stuart told me that years ago."

"Don't judge everyone according to him, honey."

Meaning Rogan. Lee hugged Charmaine and it felt good. "Thanks for looking after me, Mom. I'm glad we had these few days."

The older woman touched Lee's cheek. "Consider my offer to babysit—before you sign any papers, okay? It's time I put away my scissors at the hair salon anyway."

Lee smiled. "You're too young to retire. Besides, I've got more than one plan in the works." She had given a lot of thought to this new venture in her life. She had no idea where it would lead, only that it was the right thing to do for the baby.

Yes, she would miss Sky Dash. Terribly so. She'd miss touching the clouds, and seeing the sun glint off her wingtips. She would miss the sensation of reaching the top of the world, of...*soaring.* What she hadn't told her mother yet was that once the sale money transferred into her account, she planned to open an antique shop. And she'd begin by selling her father's teapot.

A vehicle sounded outside. Lee peered through the gauzy curtain covering the narrow side window. "What on earth would Lucien Duvall be wanting with you?" As the man climbed from his ancient pickup, she headed outside. "Hey, Lucien."

"Lee." A nod to the woman on the stoop. "Charmaine."

"Lucien," her mother said pleasantly. "To what do we owe this visit?"

"Came to see Lee." He slid a large box from the truck seat. "Thought you might want to show the...the tyke this one day. It's an album Oliver's mother put together when he was a babe."

She took the box from his bear-paw hands with their jagged fingernails. Hands of a hard-working man.

Hands Oliver had inherited, and whose DNA may be forming tiny fingers and palms this instant. Lee's eyes stung. "Thank you, Lucien."

Charmaine walked forward. "That was a nice thing to do, Lu." She touched the box, looked up at the man gazing down at her. Lee caught the exchange and felt something arc between them. An old history.

Suddenly, his smile changed his features. "Guess we're gonna be related, after all, huh, Char?"

"Yeah," she said reciprocating his delight. "Who woulda thought?"

"Well," he said, nodding to Lee. "Take care."

"You, too."

They watched him return to his truck. With a lift of his fingers, he backed from the lane and drove away.

"What was *that* about?" Lee asked, as her mother stared down the road.

"A long time ago he wanted to marry me."

"What?" Lee's jaw fell. "But he's been…" *Such an ogre and grumpy old man.*

"I know what he's been, Lee. He wasn't always. Once he was very sweet, a gentle giant."

Lee studied her mother. "He loved you."

"Yes. And I treated him very badly. All a long time ago, of course. But this is a small island and memories don't fade well here." She exhaled heavily. "I was in love with someone else."

"Steven Tait?"

In the morning sunlight, Charmaine's eyes were a crystal blue. She touched Lee's hair. "It's so bright, just like his."

"Like yours, you mean." Her father had light brown

hair. At least he did in the few photos Lee had viewed from the collection Charmaine kept in the shoebox stored in her closet. Suddenly, Lee narrowed her eyes. "Is Lucien Kat's father?"

"No."

"Are you sure? God, I'm sorry." Lee looked away. "That came out wrong, Mom."

"Don't worry about it." Charmaine's lips curved. "Will you see Rogan today? He called this morning, you know."

"Here?" Lee's heart leaped. He hadn't forgotten her. He hadn't written her off. And then another thought invaded. It had taken three days for him to call.

"You were at the clinic," Charmaine said. "He's very worried."

She had no comeback, except to say, "Why didn't you tell me when I got home?"

"You were here barely ten minutes before Lucien showed up."

Lee hugged the album to her chest. She wasn't quite ready to get in her Jeep. "What did Rogan want?"

"To talk to you."

"Did you tell him I'm fine?"

"I told him you'd see him when you got to your apartment. He's at his office," Charmaine added.

Lee closed her eyes, recalling the last moment at the farmhouse. *Worried whether I'll still marry you?* he'd asked in that deep, quiet voice, and she'd wanted to shout, *Yes!*

But she was afraid—even now, even though she knew their relationship ended when she walked off that porch.

"I can't see him," she told Charmaine.

"Honey—"

"Mom, don't interfere. Please."

"All right." Charmaine folded her arms. "But I will say this. Long ago I made a choice and my life took a different turn. One that was harder than I ever expected." She gripped Lee's hand. "Don't do what I did, Lee. Make your choice from here." She pressed a hand to her breastbone. "Your heart knows best. Always." With that, her mother walked back into the house.

A slight wind rustled the evergreens and oaks bordering the driveway. Lee remained where she stood. She carried another man's child, but loved a man whose past would haunt her forever. And she adored *his* child.

Don't do what I did.

Charmaine's words spurred her forward. The last thing she wanted was to follow her mother's footsteps.

Chapter Thirteen

Lee checked her e-mail on the Sky Dash Web site the moment she returned to her apartment. While at her mother's place, she'd reviewed upcoming flight inquiries from her laptop and scheduled three honeymoon tours for Memorial Day weekend. Today's inquiries presented two bookings for June and four in July.

She was typing a reply to the last when a knock sounded.

Rogan stood on the other side of the peephole.

Her heart fluttered. *He's here.*

Swinging the door open, she took in his impeccable pearl-gray shirt and dark tie, his trimmed black hair, those compelling gray eyes— Her breath staggered.

"Hey." The mouth she'd kissed a hundred times last

Monday night towed into a crooked smile. "I saw your car out back…"

Muscles limp, heart defenseless, she drank him in. "I came home an hour ago."

"You went to the clinic this morning."

His eyes brimmed with questions, and so she offered the only answer she could, the one he deserved. "We're both fine."

Relief had him exhaling slowly. "That's good, Lee. Real good to hear."

Still, she made no move to invite him in. What could she say that she hadn't already told him, that they hadn't discussed?

Five enormously long seconds passed before he stepped forward and tugged her to him, and she pressed her face against his shirt, drawing in his scent, one she'd recognize blindfolded.

"This week's been hell," he murmured into her hair. "I didn't sleep, I thought about you all the time. I dialed your number a million times, then disconnected at the last second…."

Oh, God. Me, too, me, too. Her arms slid around his waist, her nose stung when his kisses rained her temple.

"Lee, please. Let's—"

She stepped from the warmth of his body. She needed distance to say what she had rehearsed since she made her decision. "Rogan, our pasts are too intertwined, too volatile. Your wife and daughter… You'll never look at me without thinking of them." She shook her head, held up a hand when he wanted to interrupt. "I've given this a lot of thought." And more often than not cried herself to sleep in the process. "It won't work," she said.

"I'm dropping the suit against Abner."

Surprise caught her. "What on earth for?"

"I won't lose you over it."

"No." She moved farther away, gripped the door with both hands. "Don't do this. You deserve compensation. I wish—"

"You were never at fault."

"I don't want to talk about this anymore."

She started to close the door, but he laid a palm against the wood. "I need to know, Lee. Are you selling Sky Dash?"

"Where'd you hear that?"

"As you once said, it's a small island. Are you selling so Hershel can't take the plane from you in a resettlement?"

"I don't give a damn about my ex. I'm selling so I can buy a business that lets me stay home with my baby." A little antique shop Charmaine could manage during Lee's maternity leave. A shop housing a nursery in the back room while she worked. "Besides, it's a done deal." She looked askance, unwilling to meet his gaze. "I'm meeting the buyer Monday."

There was a moment's interlude. "A child and a seaplane *can* mix, Lee."

Her breath caught. Was he aware what he'd voiced? *A child and a seaplane can mix…?* She wanted to burst into tears.

He touched her cheek. "We can work this out. I know we can."

We. If he didn't leave soon, she'd be a puddle on the floor. "I need you to go," she whispered, ushering him out.

"Lee, please…"

"*Go.*"

Alone again, she set her forehead against the door, and listened to his footsteps descend the stairs. When quiet returned, she slid down the wood until her rump hit the floor. Hugging her knees, she put her face into her arms and cried. For him, for her, for the mess life had tossed them, a mess she couldn't seem to see beyond.

From his office window the following Monday morning, Rogan viewed the clouds stockpiling beyond the cove. Dockside, Lee readied her plane. *Now or never,* he thought, snatching a black windbreaker from the coat tree. On the landing, he flipped the sign to Closed, and hurried down the stairs.

Outside, a breeze carried the cold smell of rain. As always, seagulls navigated the air currents, seeking whatever marine life swam the dark waters lapping the wharf. May had arrived with barely a hint of sunshine or warmth.

A small shiver traveled Rogan's skin. He didn't care for Lee flying in weather that could change in a heartbeat.

Except she'd done it a thousand times. Reminding himself of that, he broke into a jog when he saw Fitz store the last of the packages into the cargo hold and Lee give a "See you later" wave.

"Lee," Rogan called, sprinting the last hundred feet.

Her head snapped in his direction.

He halted in front of her. She looked wonderful. Green eyes sparking fire, freckles gold as sugar granules. "We need to talk."

"Aren't you working today?" she asked, peering over his shoulder toward the marine walkway.

"Office is closed until tomorrow." He attempted a grin. "CEOs can take time off any day."

"Well," she said, storing the anchor rope on the floor behind the pilot's chair. "I can't." With two nimble steps, she ascended into the cockpit. "Call me tonight if you still need to talk."

He couldn't wait until then. Today, she meant to see the Bremerton buyer interested in Sky Dash.

A raindrop struck Rogan's face. At anchor, the seaplane bobbed on the water. Before he reconsidered his options, he stepped across the narrow strip of water, onto the pontoon, squeezed behind her chair, and settled in the passenger's seat beside Lee.

"What are you doing?" Her eyes flashed irritation.

"Coming with you," he replied as he reached for the second headset—and grinned at her.

"You can't come along. I have work to do."

Leaning across the space between their seats, he gave her a smacking kiss on the mouth. "So do I. Now crank that damn propeller and let's get the show on the road."

She made a gesture at the windscreen where rain had started to spit. "Look at the weather, Rogan. You have enough trouble flying when conditions are perfect. This is *not* a good idea."

His eyes held hers for an extended moment. "I'll be fine, Lee. Besides, I listened to the forecast. They're expecting a few showers. Nothing major."

"On the ground, yes. Up a half mile, it's a whole other ballgame. If you're trying to prove something—"

"I trust you," he said quietly. "Always have."

He watched her swallow. Finally, she pushed the Start button, initiated the engine and spoke to the Seattle tower. Guiding the craft out into the cove, she recited her instrument check.

With a conscious effort, Rogan kept his hands loose on his thighs. The seaplane picked up speed against the wind and bounced across the chop before lifting into the air. When his gut dropped to his toes, he forced back the constriction in his throat.

While he told himself the flight was no different than the others he'd taken, it didn't settle his insides any less. There was more at stake. Along with Danny, there was Lee. And with Lee came a love, a *passion,* beyond anything Rogan had previously known.

As the plane climbed, he looked over at the woman manning the controls. This morning, she'd bundled her red hair into a captivating mess atop her head. Strands poked from a big white clip, and straggled down her nape. More than anything, he wanted to twist a kinky lock around his finger—the way he'd done when they lay in bed. When she lay above him.

"So." Her voice sluiced through his memories. "What did you want to talk about?"

"Dan wants a puppy."

She let out a half laugh, half snort. "That is not why you boarded this plane."

"Maybe it isn't the exact reason, but Dan does want to know if you'll help pick from this litter he knows about." Rogan looked at Lee. "I had hoped we'd go this past weekend, but…"

"I wasn't available."

Below his window, shoreline and hills fell steadily away. His stomach wanted to fall with them. "Maybe we could go tonight."

She studied the instrument panel. "Why else are you paying for this trip?"

"You're hoping to sell Sky Dash today."

A frown etched her brow. "Did I say that?"

"When you were angry with me last Friday."

"Oh." She checked her side window. "Well, I'm still mad at you."

Except she didn't sound mad. He took heart. "I told you then, and I'll say it again, we can work this out." The aircraft dipped, suspending his stomach somewhere in the stratosphere. "Unghhh," he groaned. "I don't believe selling is—" another dip "—the answer."

"It'll get me the money I require for my child's future," she said reasonably.

They were out of the cove, aiming for the Sound when the plane suddenly plunged twenty feet. In the next instant, a gust of wind caught its underbelly and rocked the craft like a ghastly cradle.

"Whoa!" Rogan forgot to breathe, forgot to close his eyes or look at the floor-well between his feet. Too late he shot a peek out the side window separating him from three thousand feet of air and a cold black surface of water.

The coffee he'd bought at Coffee Sense thirty minutes ago flirted with the base of his tongue.

"Don't be afraid." Lee's voice, a soft murmur, a lifeline in his ear. "It's only a bit of air turbulence. Normal with this cloud cover."

Above the roar and sway of the plane, he noticed how easily her hands maintained the controls, the quiet in her voice, the composure on her features.

Lee Tait was a consummate pilot. The thought of her giving up her profession tore a hole through Rogan.

He recalled her determination the morning of Addie's leg cramp, her composure the day Danny broke through the hayloft floor.

Thanks for saving me, his son had told her.

She'd done more than that, Rogan realized. *She's saved me.* She'd hauled him from the void of his life, freed him of his guilt and heartbreak in the wake of Darby's and Sophie's tragedy.

"We're almost through it." Her melodic voice sang into the headset.

He tried to chuckle and instead tasted his breakfast. "Well, I can't say you didn't warn me. As usual, I should've listened."

Her fingers closed briefly over his left fist. "Don't beat yourself up over hindsight."

The plane dipped and shuddered and creaked. "Seems I've been doing that for three years." When the plane leveled again, he turned to catch her gaze. "I'm tired of it."

She was about to respond when the aircraft plunged fast as a bucket of bricks from a five-story building.

Flung back in the seat, Rogan seized the armrests. Danny would be an orphan after all. Rogan could see it plain as the dark foggy cloud mass they traveled through. *OhGodohGod.*

"Hang on," Lee told him. "It's almost over."

Over. When they'd barely begun.

Over for him and Danny and Lee.

"Lee—" His teeth chattered; he couldn't get another thought together. Damn it, when would his fear of flying end? He was sick of it. Sick of the paranoia, the nightmare, the helplessness.

Something hot surged through his chest. *No more. No. More.* "When this is done—" The Cessna rattled and bucked and booted his words into the abyss below.

"I'm here, Rogan," Lee soothed. "Don't be afraid."

A light clicked in his brain. Not fear…anger. For years anger had manifested into fear.

He'd been angry with Darby for taking Sophie on that death trip. And Abner Air for their role in the crash. But most of all because he'd deemed work more important than his family that day.

Suddenly, Rogan shook his head. "Lee," he said, feeling free of a thirty-eight-month weight. "I'm not afraid. Not anymore. And this isn't over. It's just beginning. *We're* just beginning."

Had they been on the ground and not in the clouds, he would've taken her face in his hands. Oh, but he wanted to wrap her up like a beautiful jewel and tuck her into his heart. "I want another chance, honey. With you. Because, damn it, we *are* going to make it."

At that moment, the seaplane broke through the clouds and flew into sunshine, and Rogan laughed again. "There," he said. "Do you believe me?"

An auburn brow lifted. "Do I have a choice?"

"Nope." He couldn't contain the goofy grin. The plane began its descent and approach to Bremerton. They were a team, he and Lee. As a team they could get through anything, including operating Sky Dash, and raising two—or more—children in a house filled with love, on a quiet country road.

Rogan waited until she finished her dialogue with the control tower and taxied to the pier. The plane finally in position for anchoring, he unbuckled his belt, removed his headgear, eager to kiss the woman he loved beyond reason.

She set a hand on his chest, her eyes shining with spring brightness. "Was that anxiety talking back there? Or did you mean what you said?"

"Every word," he said softly.

A smile bloomed. "I'm so glad for you, Rogan."

He wanted to kiss her, but he had to ask again. "Do you love me?"

She looked away. "What I feel isn't important."

He turned her face gently so they were inches apart. "Do you?" he repeated.

"You know I do," she whispered. "I've said it, remember?"

He did. "Do you trust me?"

"Why wouldn't I?"

"Because I don't want you to sell Sky Dash. We can do this together, honey. As a team, as a family. But, you need to trust me the way I've trusted you whenever I'm in this plane—and whenever you're with my son. You need to trust our love, Lee." His hand cupped her cheek, and he set his mouth tenderly on hers. "Marry me. Build a home and a future for our children. For us."

A tear tracked her cheek. "How? If I don't sell this business I'll have no investment for the future."

He smiled. "Trust me, sweetheart. Trust in us."

She hung on his gaze. "Okay."

One ordinary, everyday word. It held his universe.

Rogan kissed her. Eons later, he lifted his head and chuckled. "I think we've drifted a little."

Through the windscreen, past the propeller, the dock lay ten feet away.

Lee laughed. "Well, considering we're pointed in the right direction… Ready to fly home again?"

Fly home. The best two words Rogan heard in years.

"You bet."

Epilogue

December, the same year...

She stood at the base of the porch steps and surveyed the strings of colorful lights her family purchased that afternoon.

Her family. She loved the sound. Rogan, Danny, Olivia. *Hers.*

Lee smiled. Dad and son had spent the last hour coiling the lights around the porch's pillars and along the top of the railing, while she tacked big red bows on the corner post of the stairs and hung a cheerful wreath on the front door.

"Look, Olivia," she whispered to the baby bundled close as cotton candy in the pink sling against Lee's chest. "Your first Christmas lights." Dark blue eyes stared up at Lee.

"She awake?" Rogan came down the steps. As always, his grin took her breath.

Tonight, she thought. Tonight they would make love again. Today's appointment at the clinic settled the question and, after months of abstinence, she couldn't wait for the next three hours to pass. Oh, yes. Tonight she'd surprise him with the diaphanous bit of lingerie she'd picked up last week in Seattle. Picturing his expression when he saw the scrap of black, she smiled deeply.

"What are you grinning at?" he asked, setting his mouth against hers and lingering, before he kissed Olivia's rosy cheek.

Suddenly abashed, Lee slid her gaze away. "Just being happy."

So much had happened since that day in early May after they'd flown through the batch of air turbulence. That day her mission had been to sell her plane—until Rogan gave her another option.

After calling off the buyer, she talked to Peyton Sawyer. Flying full-time for Sky Dash? How could he *not* take the offer? Five minutes from home, and with Lee taking the hassles of operative administration in her apartment-turned-office, the job was perfect.

Shortly thereafter, on a sunny June Saturday following the birth of Addie's son, Lee and Rogan spoke their vows under the old oak.

Kat, Addie, Skip and Johnny—with Danny bearing a pair of golden rings—stood beside them. A smattering of family and friends watched from chairs scattered across the grass. Charmaine had cried and Lucien had handed her a hanky.

"*You* make me happy," Rogan said, kissing her again. "I can't wait for the doctor's go-ahead."

Hiding her smile, Lee nuzzled Olivia. Some things were worth keeping secret for a little while. "Think Danny needs help with the hot chocolate?"

Moments ago, their son—she thought of the little boy as hers now—had gone inside to make three mugs of the winter drink.

"Nah." Rogan tugged Lee into his arms. "He's an old hand at brewing the stuff. You taught him well."

She rested her head against her husband's shoulder. "The lights are beautiful, Rogan."

Before he could reply, Danny and his Lab/shepherd pup, Inky, rushed through the front door.

"Dad, Mom," the boy whispered excitedly. "Look over there."

Turning in the direction he indicated, Lee let out a soft, *"Ohh."*

At a distance of a hundred yards, on the pasture knoll, a doe and half-grown fawn grazed side by side in the twilight. But it wasn't the sight of the deer stinging Lee's eyes. Danny had called her Mom.

"Oh, Danny," she said. "They're beautiful."

He came to stand beside them. "I saw 'em from the greenhouse window when I was picking mint for the hot chocolates." His grin stretched ear to ear. "October Farm is the coolest place."

Hugging Lee close, Rogan drew their son against them. "That's because we're a cool family, son."

"Yeah," Danny whispered, petting the pup at his

feet. "We're the coolest, awesomest family in the whole wide world."

Awesomest family. Lee couldn't agree more. With the warmth of her husband and children enveloping her, she watched the doe lift her head, elongated ears erect, dark eyes centered on them.

One family in harmony with the other.

A lovely omen.

* * * * *

Don't miss Kat's story, the next chapter in Mary J. Forbes's new miniseries HOME TO FIREWOOD ISLAND. *On sale soon, wherever Silhouette Books are sold.*

Here is a sneak preview of
A STONE CREEK CHRISTMAS,
the latest in Linda Lael Miller's acclaimed
McKETTRICK *series.*

A lonely horse brought vet Olivia O'Ballivan to
Tanner Quinn's farm, but it's the rancher's love
that might cause her to stay.

A STONE CREEK CHRISTMAS
Available December 2008
from Silhouette Special Edition.

Tanner heard the rig roll in around sunset. Smiling, he wandered to the window. Watched as Olivia O'Ballivan climbed out of her Suburban, flung one defiant glance toward the house and started for the barn, the golden retriever trotting along behind her.

Taking his coat and hat down from the peg next to the back door, he put them on and went outside. He was used to being alone, even liked it, but keeping company with Doc O'Ballivan, bristly though she sometimes was, would provide a welcome diversion.

He gave her time to reach the horse Butterpie's stall, then walked into the barn.

The golden retriever came to greet him, all wagging tail and melting brown eyes, and he bent to stroke her soft, sturdy back. "Hey, there, dog," he said.

Sure enough, Olivia was in the stall, brushing Butterpie down and talking to her in a soft, soothing voice that touched something private inside Tanner and made him want to turn on one heel and beat it back to the house.

He'd be damned if he'd do it, though.

This was *his* ranch, *his* barn. Well-intentioned as she was, *Olivia* was the trespasser here, not him.

"She's still very upset," Olivia told him, without turning to look at him or slowing down with the brush.

Shiloh, always an easy horse to get along with, stood contentedly in his own stall, munching away on the feed Tanner had given him earlier. Butterpie, he noted, hadn't touched her supper as far as he could tell.

"Do you know anything at all about horses, Mr. Quinn?" Olivia asked.

He leaned against the stall door, the way he had the day before, and grinned. He'd practically been raised on horseback; he and Tessa had grown up on their grandmother's farm in the Texas hill country, after their folks divorced and went their separate ways, both of them too busy to bother with a couple of kids. "A few things," he said. "And I mean to call you Olivia, so you might as well return the favor and address me by my first name."

He watched as she took that in, dealt with it, decided on an approach. He'd have to wait and see what that turned out to be, but he didn't mind. It was a pleasure just watching Olivia O'Ballivan grooming a horse.

"All right, *Tanner,*" she said. "This barn is a disgrace. When are you going to have the roof fixed? If it snows again, the hay will get wet and probably mold…"

He chuckled, shifted a little. He'd have a crew out there the following Monday morning to replace the roof and shore up the walls—he'd made the arrangements over a week before—but he felt no particular compunction to explain that. He was enjoying her ire too much; it made her color rise and her hair fly when she turned her head, and the faster breathing made her perfect breasts go up and down in an enticing rhythm. "What makes you so sure I'm a greenhorn?" he asked mildly, still leaning on the gate.

At last she looked straight at him, but she didn't move from Butterpie's side. "Your hat, your boots—that fancy red truck you drive. I'll bet it's customized."

Tanner grinned. Adjusted his hat. "Are you telling me real cowboys don't drive red trucks?"

"There are lots of trucks around here," she said. "Some of them are red, and some of them are new. And *all* of them are splattered with mud or manure or both."

"Maybe I ought to put in a car wash, then," he teased. "Sounds like there's a market for one. Might be a good investment."

She softened, though not significantly, and spared him a cautious half smile, full of questions she probably wouldn't ask. "There's a good car wash in Indian Rock," she informed him. "People go there. It's only forty miles."

"Oh," he said with just a hint of mockery. "*Only* forty miles. Well, then. Guess I'd better dirty up my truck if I want to be taken seriously in these here parts. Scuff up my boots a bit, too, and maybe stomp on my hat a couple of times."

Her cheeks went a fetching shade of pink. "You are twisting what I said," she told him, brushing Butterpie again, her touch gentle but sure. "I meant…"

Tanner envied that little horse. Wished he had a furry hide, so he'd need brushing, too.

"You *meant* that I'm not a real cowboy," he said. "And you could be right. I've spent a lot of time on construction sites over the last few years, or in meetings where a hat and boots wouldn't be appropriate. Instead of digging out my old gear, once I decided to take this job, I just bought new."

"I bet you don't even *have* any old gear," she challenged, but she was smiling, albeit cautiously, as though she might withdraw into a disapproving frown at any second.

He took off his hat, extended it to her. "Here," he teased. "Rub that around in the muck until it suits you."

She laughed, and the sound—well, it caused a powerful and wholly unexpected shift inside him. Scared the hell out of him and, paradoxically, made him yearn to hear it again.

* * * * *

Discover how this rugged rancher's wanderlust
is tamed in time for a merry Christmas, in
A STONE CREEK CHRISTMAS.
In stores December 2008.

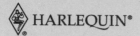

HARLEQUIN®

American ★ Romance®

HOLLY JACOBS
Once Upon a Christmas

Daniel McLean is thrilled to learn he
may be the father of Michelle Hamilton's
nephew. When Daniel starts to spend
time with Brandon and help her organize
Erie Elementary's big Christmas Fair, the
three discover a paternity test won't make
them a family, but the love they discover
just might….

Available December 2008
wherever books are sold.

LOVE, HOME & HAPPINESS

HARLEQUIN® *Romance*®

Marry-Me Christmas

by *USA TODAY* bestselling author

SHIRLEY JUMP

A *Bride* FOR ALL *Seasons*

Ruthless and successful journalist Flynn never mixes business with pleasure. But when he's sent to write a scathing review of Samantha's bakery, her beauty and innocence catches him off guard. Has this small-town girl unlocked the city slicker's heart?

Available December 2008.

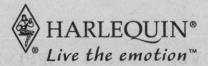

HARLEQUIN®
Live the emotion™

HR17557

REQUEST YOUR FREE BOOKS!
2 FREE NOVELS PLUS 2 FREE GIFTS!

SPECIAL EDITION®
Life, Love and Family!

SSE08R